THE INHERITANCE

A PORT HENRY NOVEL

AMY BRIGGS

The Inheritance
By Amy Briggs

Cover Design by Kristen Hope Mazzola
Editing by All About the Edits

❄ Created with Vellum

For all those animal lovers who didn't intend to be.

CHAPTER 1

DONOVAN

Spring was coming to an end in Port Henry, an affluent seaside town roughly two hours northeast of New York City, and with the change of seasons, a transition in the ambiance of the community. As summer approached, the quiet of the square would shift to a bustling tourist trap and the locals who resided there year-round would either saddle up for an overtly profitable spell through fall, or they'd hide out and grumble as the weekenders and seasonal residents descended from the city.

Donovan Hunter was a local, but he wasn't one of the natives who purchased an opulent home, established residency, and invited celebrities and socialites to parties all season, nor did he inherit a big house from a wealthy family. The old money was an entirely different breed altogether, and they had a firm policy of not letting the new money take over wherever possible. A distinct divide existed in the community, which wasn't apt to change.

While he had spent most of his life in the Port, Donovan was neither old nor new money. In fact, he'd grown up with very little. The only son of a single mother, he spent his formidable years attending the one and only public school in the area while his mother cleaned the houses of both the long-standing residents as well as some of the more contemporary, newer folks. The subset of the working class on the shorefront was largely a group that didn't plan to stay long and, with the exception of a handful of his classmates, when the time came, Donovan couldn't wait to leave for college as well.

But, as often happens with the sons of hard-working mothers, Donovan found himself back in Port Henry after graduating, hustling all summer each year at odd jobs and serving at high-end restaurants to put himself through veterinary school. Besides his mother, Maggie, their pets had been the only other reason he came back. By the time he finally graduated from veterinary school, he'd established himself as a small-town celebrity of sorts among the working class, at least the ones with pets.

Opening his own practice had always been a dream, and though he didn't think he'd do it in Port Henry, it was the only true home he'd ever known. Any resentment he'd felt toward the wealthy had waned as he treated sick pups of the rich and famous, helped mend the semi-exotic felines who found themselves in precarious situations, and tended to the other random animals people chose to keep as pets.

By the time he was thirty, he'd become the top veterinarian in the area, even being named one of the "Top 40 Under 40" in *Long Island Magazine*. He was well-known for his bedside manner with the animals, but also after years of being in the employ of the well-off, he knew how to appease them and their demanding ways with a smile. It didn't hurt his cause that he was also good-looking. So handsome that, on numerous occasions, actors, directors, and wannabe somebodies had tried to get him to attend their parties under the guise of their thanks for his work, but also to recruit him for parts in movies, television shows, and only God knew what else.

He was always flattered, and couldn't help his flirtatious personality, but the phony nature of most of his clients wasn't particularly a turn on. That didn't stop him from the usual annual summer flings. He was, after all, still a man, and the dating pool in Port Henry wasn't exactly a hotbed of dateable singles looking for monogamy. He gave as good as he got, and every summer brought a few of the same ladies by with their dogs that weren't really sick or their cats with anxiety over the travel to their summer home. There was always one or two new acquaintances to make though too, even if only for the evening here and there.

Donovan reflected on the approaching summer with a grin. It had been a while since he'd had any fun and the new crop of women coming to town with their plunging necklines, short skirts, unfriendly dogs, and vacation state of mind was about to begin. The summer crowd kept his business thriving, and his sheets warm. What more could a thirty-two-year-old bachelor want?

The last patient of the day was a Bengal cat that was walking with a limp. Mrs. Forbes, who was pushing her mid-sixties and had a bit of a limp herself, had brought "Princess Dinah of the Nile" in on a leash.

"Mrs. Forbes, why is Dinah on a leash today if her paw is hurt?" he asked, annoyed the poor animal wasn't in a crate.

"Now, Dr. Hunter, you know that Her Majesty does not

like getting stuffed into that damned box. She prefers to walk, even if it is with a limp."

Mrs. Geraldine Forbes, of the Montauk Forbes, was old money. Very old money. Legend had it her late husband died a mysterious death in his fifties when Geraldine was just thirty herself. Nobody liked him. Roger Forbes was a curmudgeon at best, and an asshole on a good day. He treated everyone as if they were beneath him, and nobody that Donovan was aware of shed a tear for him, including Geraldine.

"I know that she is royalty, but if her paw is injured, we don't want her walking on it, okay?" Donovan replied softly, and patted the table between them for her to place Dinah upon.

The cat was beautiful. With huge green eyes and spots like a leopard, the domestic Bengal was small for its breed, and extremely friendly. Donovan felt animals could sense people that were into them and as such, most animals were quite friendly with him unless, of course, they were very sick or injured. Dinah was no exception and she rubbed her head against him as he examined her front paws.

"Did she fall or anything that you're aware of?" he asked.

"I don't know, dear. She's always climbing about in my closets and such, and she can jump so goddamn high, it's hard to tell. She's an explorer," Geraldine replied, shrugging her shoulders.

After he gently squeezed the cat's paws and found the reaction he was looking for, Donovan was certain it wasn't serious. "I am pretty sure it's just a sprain, Mrs. Forbes."

"It's not broken or anything?"

If it were broken, you wouldn't be able to walk her in here on a leash, he thought. "No, she didn't get terribly upset when I felt her paws, and nothing appears to be dislocated.

4

I'm going to give you some kitty ibuprofen to mix in her food twice a day, which will help with inflammation. Try to keep her from jumping too high or getting herself in any predicaments for a few days, and she'll be good as new." He paused before continuing, "She needs to go home in a carrier though. She shouldn't be walking around on that paw." He attempted to veil his irritation, internally chalking it up to Mrs. Forbes' senility.

"Okay, okay, Doctor. Tell that pretty redhead out front to box up my cat." Geraldine rolled her eyes at him. She may have been beginning her golden years, but it seemed her sass was still as sharp as a twenty-year-old's.

Donovan chuckled. "It's for the best, I promise." He lightly patted Geraldine on the forearm before giving Dinah a few more head scratches on his way out of the exam room.

"How is Her Majesty, the Queen of Sheba?" Toni asked with a grin, once they were out of earshot.

Antoinette Fournier had been Donovan's assistant and veterinary technician since the very beginning. They met briefly in high school, and then again when he came back to the Port to open his practice. She, too, had been a part of the second generation of the working class in town until she married Scott Dewey, of the Dewey Soda empire. They'd met one summer when Scott was on vacation at his family's enormous mansion on the bay, where Scott hosted many an unsupervised party for his friends.

Long since divorced, Toni didn't need to work. With young love comes the belief it will last forever, and thus no prenuptial agreement. Since Scott's father had placed several smaller, albeit profitable, businesses in his son's name, as his wife, Toni was awarded a hefty sum. Nobody knew the exact dollar amount, but to be rid of the family as a whole, she took a payout from them instead of half the businesses when her husband's philandering came to light. Because it wasn't about the money, Toni took great pleasure in her work with animals.

Donovan chuckled at her reference. "The *princess* is fine, but can you please get a carrier for Mrs. Forbes to take her home in? She has a sprained paw. She will also need six doses of the cat ibuprofen."

"You got it, Doc," she replied.

As she sauntered off to find Mrs. Forbes a cat carrier befitting royalty, Donovan couldn't help but watch her ass sway back and forth in her tight scrubs. Divorced women always had great bodies, especially when their ex-husbands footed the bill for it, and Toni was no exception. Her implants, a classy wedding gift from her former betrothed, paired with the personal trainer he was fairly certain she was fucking between sessions, kept her looking like she had the body of a twenty-something even though she was close to thirty-three. *Squats. She must be doing a lot of squats.*

Donovan shook off the thoughts of bending his assistant over the exam table and bid farewell to Mrs. Forbes and the princess. Summer would be there soon, and he'd be able to get that itch scratched from someone he wasn't paying to assist him soon enough.

Later that evening, after feeding his four cats, Hulk, Thor, Ivy, and Diana, and his two dogs Archie and Veronica, he picked up the book he was reading and took it to the porch with a bottle of beer. A storm was coming through and while the wind was picking up off the coast, the position of the small house protected him from the impending weather. Still cool enough for a sweatshirt, Donovan put his feet up on the rattan ottoman his mother had given him as a gift when he purchased the house, and gazed at the sky.

The dark clouds coming in were moving quickly but brought a refreshing and cool breeze that could only be felt close to the waterfront. Real estate in the Port was always outrageous, which was why the rich and famous, and well-to-do New Yorkers liked to vacation there. Its exclusivity brought with it a virtual billboard advertising your net worth if you could afford to spend summers there. It wasn't always the case, but most of the folks with houses had paid a pretty penny and the resale value went up year over year, creating a vacuum of the rich making each other richer with every summer season.

The house Donovan bought was a fixer-upper by every stretch of the imagination, and while larger than what he needed just for himself, was quite small relative to the area where it was located. It had gone into foreclosure, and when the bank took it back from the owner who couldn't keep up with the Joneses, he was able to snatch it up for a fraction of what it would have gone for on the market. The property alone was worth more than the house, but Donovan enjoyed working on it himself in the slow season, and it had become a home he loved, even if it was in a town he wasn't always sure he felt the same way about.

CHAPTER 2

RILEY

N ew York City was bustling as always and Riley Maxwell could hear the horns blaring from the hostile drivers sitting in rush hour traffic, trying to get home. "I wonder if they know that honking your horn is illegal in New York City," she said.

"Is it really?" Jameson Prescott, her client on the other end of the phone, replied.

"Yes. Unless it's an emergency, of course, nobody is supposed to honk their horns at all." She mused at the useless knowledge that filled her active mind.

"You should be on that trivia game show. You'd probably win." Jameson chuckled.

"Now, you know that I don't like to be out and about. That sounds pretty out and about to me," she replied. She wasn't officially diagnosed agoraphobic, but she didn't enjoy leaving the confines of her apartment for more than a food run most of the time. It wasn't that she was afraid to go out, more that the interactions she had left a lot to be desired. She found strangers exasperating and having had little experience socializing with the type of work she did, it hadn't gotten much better after college.

Her favorite client, Mr. Prescott, had hired her to help him write his memoirs. Jameson Prescott was probably about her dad's age she guessed. Older than her, somewhere around his mid-fifties, he'd lived an interesting life and wanted to leave a legacy of some kind behind. Not for his family, as he didn't have any, but he didn't want to be forgotten. That's what he told Riley when they met for the first time in person, at Riley's favorite coffee shop three blocks from her apartment. She appreciated his candor and the fact that he had a story to tell–an interesting one thus far as well.

"You're young, Riley. You really need to get out of that apartment and get some fresh air," he said in a fatherly tone.

"Okay, *Dad*, I'll take that under advisement," she replied sarcastically.

"I know that means you won't."

"You know me better than I thought you did, Jameson," she replied with a laugh.

The two had grown to be friends over the eighteen months they'd been working together on his project. Asking someone to explain their life in detail so it can be documented meant the two of them spent a tremendous amount of time talking. Riley was never quite sure how Jameson found her, but she was grateful for the opportunity and had been paid a very large sum of money to make herself available on Jameson's timeline. He had requested she name a dollar amount that would be sufficient enough for her to decline any other large projects and only take on small, creative projects while under contract with him.

Originally, Riley thought it was a joke and she named what she believed was a fair amount that equated to a full year's salary for a mid-level copywriter. Not only did Jameson agree to it immediately, but he also gave her a ten-thousand-dollar bonus—he called it—for beginning right away and wrapping up any projects she currently had on her plate. She signed the contract with him, and when the money was wired to her account almost instantly, she realized he was not only serious, he was rich.

What she didn't know when she first met him was what a kind soul he was, and that he'd lived a life worth telling the story of. When they were introduced face to face shortly after finalizing the contract, Jameson made the trip to New York City and took her out for the fanciest dinner she'd ever had. That was the only other time they'd met. It had been over a year since they'd gotten together in person, and although she generally preferred working remotely with all of her clients, she was compelled to ask him to come back.

"Do you remember the first time that we met in person?" she asked him.

"Of course I do. Why do you ask?" he replied.

"I was just thinking it's been a long time, and we've been working together for over a year, almost daily. Maybe we should sit down and go over everything we have for the book. Start talking about how you want to lay it out, and all that?" There was no reason for her to ask other than the fact she simply wanted to see him. She enjoyed his company, and they had the most interesting conversations. It was unusual for Riley to request a sit-down. She'd never even considered asking that a meeting take place in the same time zone, let alone the same room.

Silence on the line had Riley reconsidering. "I mean, we

don't have to. I just thought it might be nice," she added with a shake to her voice.

"I'm sorry, no, that would be lovely," Jameson replied. "I'll be away on business for a while though, so we'll have to plan it for some time this summer. That's actually why I called you today. I need to take a short break on the book while I'm gone and we can get back to it when I return. That will be a perfect time for us to look at everything with fresh eyes, and you can come up to Port Henry if you'd like."

Riley hadn't considered going up to the Port. She assumed he would come back to the city. Spending even an afternoon there would be wonderful, and she immediately began racking her brain to see if she could turn it into a mini-vacation. "That would be lovely, Jameson! Are you sure though? I don't want to be an imposition." She knew some might think their relationship was intimate and to an extent, it was, but it was also intellectual. She didn't feel anything but kinship with him and she was quite certain it was the same for him.

Besides the age difference between them, Jameson was practically old enough to be her father, and he was more of a mentor in the ways of life—an advisor, of sorts. Trying to qualify their relationship in a way that was both platonic and special rarely crossed her mind, except for the times she tried to explain it to her best friend, Colette, who lived in Boston. Colette finally chalked Riley's fascination with the older man as filling a void the crappy relationship she had with her father had left.

"I think we're long past the formalities, Riley. You know more about me and my life than any of my wives ever did at this point." He laughed. "It's also no secret that I have a house too big for just the likes of me, and you're welcome here anytime. I think a summer get together in the Port would do us both some good, don't you?"

"I'd love that. In the meantime, are there any other projects you would like me to work on while you're away?" Riley was employed by him and only him, so if she wasn't working on the book, she wasn't really clear what he wanted her to be doing with her time, and she didn't want to take advantage of the payment she'd received.

"Just reread what we have and make any notes you think I need to see."

"Are you sure that's all you want me to do?" she asked. It didn't seem like enough work, although they had pages and pages of notes and only a few chapters compiled in readable book form even after all the time they'd spent working on it.

"I'm sure," he replied. "Take a little time off to enjoy spring in the city. Even in that concrete jungle, there are leaves that change with the passing of time."

Confused, but not altogether upset about a little time away from her desk, she agreed. "When should I expect you back?"

"If all goes well, I should be back home in the Port in about three weeks."

"Where you headed?"

"Switzerland," he replied without further explanation.

"Gonna do any skiing while you're there?" she asked. Riley had never been skiing but assumed it was something you'd do if you were headed to Switzerland. She hadn't traveled much, but her mom used to tell her that living in New York City was almost as good. With the different parts of the city, like Chinatown, Little Brazil, and so many other ethnically rich areas, you could go on a tour of the world within just a few blocks. She knew it wasn't the same, but smiled reminiscing about her mom's imagination.

"No, no. I don't ski. I have some business to attend to. But I'll be in touch," he said.

"Okay, sounds good. I'll follow up with you next week with any thoughts I have, and then we'll regroup and plan a visit when you get back. Have a great time."

"Thank you, Riley, I'll try."

A WEEK HAD GONE by and Riley tried to honor Jameson's request, but "going out and getting fresh air" as he'd suggested wasn't specific enough for her. She didn't know what to do with herself. After college, where she'd met her best friend, she started working immediately and hadn't had much of a social life. The people in New York she knew the best were the shop owners around her block. Not much of a joiner, Riley had a hard time making friends, and if it weren't for being placed together as roommates freshman year, she and Colette never would have become friends either. As luck would have it though, they hit it off and stayed close, even with the distance between them geographically after graduating.

Riley was bored and with two more weeks without her work buddy, she knew she had to find something productive to do with her time, so she checked out her latest requests for freelance work and decided to pick up a couple of small jobs to occupy her time. Graduating at the top of her class with excellent communication skills, she'd managed to work freelance writing almost immediately and had developed a loyal and robust client base. She may have been an introvert in her personal life, but professionally, Riley was dynamic and had the skills and work ethic to have her own business at a young age.

Now thirty, she had her pick of jobs. She had all but taken

the last year off to work on Jameson's project, but she wasn't hurting for incoming requests. As she perused the list, she found two easy blog posts that needed to be written and emailed the clients to let them know she'd take the work on, and she would have it done within a few days. Grinning, she started to feel useful again, a sensation that kept her from wallowing in boredom or self-pity, whichever crept in first.

Able to complete the jobs relatively quickly, she took on a few more to help the time pass. Only a few times did she think she should find something to do outside her apartment, but the moments passed quickly enough that she didn't give them a second thought, and continued to hole herself up inside.

By the end of the second week, Riley hadn't left her apartment once. Finally, she decided she needed to stretch her legs and go for a walk. Spring was almost over and the heat of the city would soon be too much to bear, so she grabbed her crossbody bag, put some shoes on, and headed for the elevator. Her building was located near Columbus Circle, and the area had plenty of places to walk as well as several nearby shops and restaurants. She couldn't remember when she ate last—a pitfall of making your own hours—and when she thought about it, a rumble in her stomach reminded her it had been a while and she should find some nourishment. *Preferably in the form of Chinese food,* she thought.

After filling her belly and walking off the egg rolls and lo mein, she ventured back to her apartment. Since it was only mid-afternoon on a Friday, it seemed like the perfect time for a nap. But when Riley arrived home, there was a large towering man who looked to be in his mid to late fifties standing in front of her door. Panic set in and Riley wasn't sure whether to go back down to the lobby or confront the man. While she stood, frozen, trying to figure out why he was there, he spoke up.

"Ms. Maxwell?" he asked.

"Who's asking?" she snarled back, trying to sound tough.

"My name is Bernard Dubois." He studied her from afar as she waited for him to continue. "I'm sorry to arrive unannounced, but I am in the employ of Mr. Jameson Prescott. He... uh... sent me."

"What do you mean, he sent you?" she snapped at him.

Bernard held up a large manila envelope she hadn't noticed and held it out. "I've been instructed to deliver this to you."

Relaxing a bit, noticing this Bernard character was seemingly harmless, she approached and took the envelope. "What is this?" she asked as she took it gently from his hand.

"It's a letter from Mr. Prescott's attorney."

"Am I in some kind of trouble?" Her confusion grew and her heart began to race.

"No, ma'am. There are instructions inside. I must be going now." He nodded and quickly walked past her toward the elevator.

Spinning around, she yelled out, "Wait! Is Mr. Prescott okay?"

Bernard bowed his head and sighed. "I'm afraid not, Ms. Maxwell. But everything you need to know is in that envelope. Best of luck to you."

With that, he disappeared, leaving her in the hallway with the unopened envelope, which simply said "Riley Maxwell" scrawled in thick, black marker.

CHAPTER 3

DONOVAN

As he listened to the dog's breathing, Donovan could hear the faintest sound of a wheeze coming from Bradley's lungs. A pooch known for his allergy issues, he was having a flare-up, and his owner, Mrs. Beverly Alderidge, had brought him in to get him checked out.

"Sounds like his hay fever isn't quite over yet, Mrs. Alderidge," he said as he plucked the stethoscope from his ears and wrapped it around his neck.

"Oh, Doctor, does he need the doggie prednisone again?" she asked.

In her late forties, Beverly Alderidge was the poster model for her peers. With fresh botox and an expensive dye job, she almost passed for mid-thirties and she certainly didn't behave like the trophy wife of a tycoon. But, she was. After twelve years of marriage, Beverly spent the better part of the summers in Port Henry without her husband, who seemed to work through it instead of enjoying the spoils. This didn't stop her from throwing lavish parties all season, and it definitely didn't stop her from trying to bed the veterinarian every chance she got. Beverly brought Bradley, a six-year-old Irish Setter in every three weeks with some sort of allergy. Likely some hypochondria brought on by her own incessant allergies.

Trying not to stare at her enormous cleavage popping out the top of her skin-tight tank top, Donovan said, "Yes, he'll need some prednisone, but you should have some left from the last time you were here, right?" He prescribed some not two weeks earlier, so there should be plenty left.

"Oh yes, I can use that?" she asked, obviously squeezing her tits together as she leaned over the table between them. Now, he couldn't help but grin, she was laying it on so thick.

"You can. Just follow the same directions as before. If you don't remember them, they're on the label."

Beverly righted herself and sauntered to the other side of the table, just inches from Donovan. He was certain her hard little nipples that could clearly be seen through her age inappropriate shirt were skimming his chest. "Do you think you could make a house call later… you know, to check up on poor Bradley?"

Mulling it over, Donovan almost took her up on the offer. He knew what a house call was, and in the case of single divorced women, or unmarried tourists, he'd probably say yes. She was close enough to his type, which was more or less any of them, so long as he didn't have to work too hard at it. But, it wasn't quite summer yet, when he would be more likely to allow that sort of thing happen, and he certainly didn't fool around with married women.

"I think Bradley will be just fine, Mrs. Aldridge. Make sure you follow the instructions and bring him back in if he isn't feeling better in a few days, okay?" He smiled at her and backed away toward the door.

"Are you sure, Doctor?" she asked, practically purring, the implication that the visit had nothing to do with the dog hanging heavy in her tone.

"I'm sure, Beverly. But you have a great summer here, and let me know if you have any problems with the dogs."

Seemingly defeated, Mrs. Aldridge let herself out of the exam room, passing Donovan more closely than she had to, her strong perfume tingling his nose. He ran his palm down his face and sighed. *And so it begins*, he thought. When he first opened his practice and his summer became full of the wealthy socialites bringing their anxiety-ridden purebreds in, the thrill of the hunt was fun. For him, it was like climbing an elitist mountain to the top and planting his flag in the uncharted lands.

These women had no idea he'd grown up as one of their servants, that his mother cleaned their homes. Most of them weren't particularly kind or thoughtful when he was a child, and it was something he'd long remember. That's not to say he was revenge banging the wealthy, but their superficial attitudes made it easier to have fun and not look back.

Besides, he thought, *it wasn't like they were looking for anything more either.*

He decided to go home and take his dogs for a walk. There was a lull in the day, and he was restless. Donovan used to look forward to summers—the carefree and hapless way that people partied, the endless revolving door of new faces. Every summer held a new adventure. A new vista to conquer. But this year, he felt different. He was less eager for the change of season and more apprehensive. *What changed?* Unable to put his finger on it, he sent Toni to lunch, and they put the closed sign in the window, along with the emergency contact number.

Once home, he was greeted by his entourage of pets, each with their own quirks. The four adolescent cats were the newest addition, and they'd been rescued from the beach where a mama cat had built a little shelter in the dunes to give birth. Toni adopted the mother after Donovan performed the spay surgery, but she didn't want to take all of the kittens. They required bottle-feeding and weaning for the first two weeks, which meant constant care, and a few of them had mild eye infections that cleared up quickly. Normally, he wouldn't have separated them from their mother; however, the eye infection may have been transmitted from her, so he felt it best to get her a new home sooner rather than later. Toni had teased him relentlessly about keeping four kittens, but he didn't care. The shelter was filled to the brim, and he wasn't going to allow them to stay homeless or live in a cage when he had a house big enough for those four, and more, if he damn well pleased.

Archie and Veronica, his two pups, wagged their tails so hard they looked as though they might lift off the ground. Donovan didn't always come home during the day, so the dogs' excitement was understandable and brought a smile to his face. As soon as he uttered the "w" word—walk—they jumped into overdrive, prancing about and barely staying still long enough to get leashes on.

The house Donovan lived in was centrally located between the various neighborhoods of the Port. He decided to follow the path toward the beachfront homes as it was a long walk and the salty scent of the ocean enticed him in that direction. Several of the homes weren't occupied just yet, but a handful had year-round renters or owners. The properties were set far enough away from each other that nobody felt crowded, but not so far that any one person had a bigger piece of beach than his neighbor.

As they continued their walk, they happened upon the butler for Jameson Prescott, who was pulling weeds at the end of the driveway. He wasn't really; he was more the caretaker of the estate, and of Mr. Prescott, but Donovan always thought he acted like a butler.

"Bernard, how are you today, sir?"

He stood up from where he was crouched and brushed the dirt off his hands down the front of his jeans. "I'm well, Doctor. Out for a lunchtime stroll on this lovely day?" Bernard smiled and extended his hand to shake Donovan's before he reached down to scratch the heads of the dogs.

"I wanted to get out of the office for a bit. It's so nice out right now, you can't beat an afternoon walk with the dogs."

"No, you sure can't." Bernard gave him a toothy grin and leaned against the nearby mailbox.

"How is Mr. Prescott doing? I haven't seen him or Scrappy in a while." Jameson Prescott adopted a Great Dane about a year prior and could be seen walking him on the beach fairly regularly. He'd grown into a massive, affectionate tail-wagger and companion for the thrice-divorced man.

"I'm sorry to say, Doctor, that Mr. Prescott passed away a few days ago." The heaviness of grief was apparent in the old man's tone. "He went on a trip to Switzerland for experimental treatment but it was too late. His cancer was too far gone at that point."

Just when Donovan thought the afternoon was looking up. While they weren't close, Jameson Prescott was a kind man and the two always spent time chatting when they ran into each other, or during Scrappy's checkups. He knew that he was sick, but hadn't realized it was as bad as it turned out to be. "I'm so sorry, Bernard. Mr. Prescott was a good man."

"That he was, Doctor."

"Did he have any family? I don't remember him ever speaking of them in our talks." Donovan was pretty sure Jameson was a committed bachelor after his failed marriages, none of which resulted in any children he recalled.

"No, none to speak of," Bernard replied.

"What will happen to the house? And to Scrappy?" *The poor puppy was probably depressed without his buddy,* Donovan thought.

"The will hasn't been read officially yet, but he left his home, his assets, and all of his belongings, including Scrappy, to someone he cared about very deeply. I hope to see her here in the next week or so. Until then, I'm taking care of things." Bernard had a hopeful gleam in his eye, and Donovan wondered who this special woman could be. *Perhaps Jameson hadn't given up on the ladies after all.*

"If there is anything that I can do to help with the pup, please don't hesitate to call me, Bernard. I'm truly sorry for your loss as well," he said.

"Thank you, sir. It's definitely going to take some getting used to," he replied.

"Will you stay on as the caretaker of the estate?" Donovan asked.

"I think that will be up to the new owner. I'm prepared to stay as long as she'll have me, and I suspect in the beginning, as she's finding her way, that she will."

"I certainly hope so. You're a part of the Port family too, ya know."

"Thank you, sir. That means a lot. I've lived here on this property for over thirty years now. I'm not quite sure what I'd do someplace else."

"Well, let's hope you don't have to find out anytime soon." Donovan felt the dogs tug at their leashes and he knew they were getting restless. "I better get back to the office. We can't have Mrs. Astor's cat waiting too long for me or I'll have to refer it to a therapist."

The two men chuckled, and Bernard tipped his ball cap at Donovan as they parted ways. On the way home to drop off his dogs, Donovan wondered who Prescott would have left everything to. *If he wasn't leaving any of it to his ex-wives, and he didn't have any children, who else could it be? Prescott was worth a small fortune, so whoever the beneficiary was, they'd be inheriting a hefty sum of money. Must be nice.*

CHAPTER 4

RILEY

R iley took the envelope inside and sat down at her desk before she opened it, knowing whatever the letter said made the news final. She sighed as she pulled out a typed letter, and a smaller, sealed envelope also fell onto the desk at the same time. As she read the words on the enclosed fancy stationery as tears formed in her eyes.

DEAR MS. MAXWELL,

Enclosed is a personal letter written to you by Jameson Prescott, Esquire, to be delivered to you upon his death. As the sole beneficiary of his estate, we ask that you make arrangements immediately to visit our office for a formal reading of his last will and testament. This matter does require some urgency, as the inhabitants of the estate are now legally in your care as well and will need to be tended to as soon as possible.

While I am sure you have many questions, we will do our best to answer them and to assist you in the transition of ownership of assets, per Mr. Prescott's wishes.

We look forward to seeing you.

Sincerely,

Annabeth Carmichael, Esq.

THE ADDRESS of the law firm was a short subway ride away from her home and Riley glanced up at the clock on the wall to see if she could go immediately. Unfortunately, it was after hours for most normal businesses, so she resolved to go downtown first thing in the morning, without an appointment.

Riley was still in shock, and read the lawyer's letter several times before remembering there was a letter from Jameson. Scrambling to open it, she didn't recognize the scrawling penmanship, as they'd only ever emailed or spoken directly. The cream-colored stationery had an embossed logo at the top of the page. A swirling "JP" was encompassed by a circle at the center, just above his words.

DEAREST RILEY,

If you are reading this letter, unfortunately, the news isn't good. I went to Switzerland not on business, but for the treatment of a rare type of bone cancer. I've been unwell for some time now and knew that the possibility I might not return existed, so I have taken precautions to ensure everything is handled, and that you are taken care of.

I'm sure this is all quite overwhelming, and I do not wish to burden you, so I have made arrangements for you to have legal counsel as well as help when you go to Port Henry. As I look back on our friendship, I have but one regret, and that is how I wasn't honest with you about my condition. In my defense, it was such a great joy to me when we'd chat that I selfishly didn't want to ruin it with talk of cancer and disease. Instead, I chose to keep our talks to the things that made us both laugh and smile.

In all my marriages, I never had children, but if I did, I'd have been the proudest man in all the world if they'd turned out to be as kind and smart as you are. Which brings me to what will happen next. Since I did not have any official heirs, I am leaving everything that was mine to you. I can only imagine your jaw is on the floor right now. I've sensed your speculation about how much money I actually had, and you will know soon—it's a lot.

There will be enough for you to travel the world, which I hope that you do, as well as take care of any financial responsibilities that you have. My home will also be yours, and everything inside. My caretaker and longtime friend, Bernard, will be waiting for you at the house in the Port, ready to help you. He has been in my service for thirty years or so and can answer most of your questions, as I'm sure there are many. As time passes, and you learn more, Bernard will be a great resource for you, and when you are ready for the rest of my story, he will be the one to provide you what you need.

Lastly, Riley, I wanted to thank you. Our friendship has meant a great deal to me, and although it began as a business transaction, you've gotten to know me better than anyone I've ever met, aside from Bernard. It has been my honor to be your friend, and in my passing, it is my honor to help take care of you and your future. I wish that I could be there to answer your questions, and to help you transition into what

most assuredly will be a bit of a strange new life, but know
that I am with you in spirit, always.

 Your loyal friend,
 Jameson Prescott

RILEY GENTLY SET the letter down on the table as the tears poured down her face. Until that very moment, she hadn't realized just how valuable her friendship with Jameson had been. The financial windfall she was to receive was so far from her conscious that she'd completely forgotten about it until she read the letter again and then one more time after that.

 I can't believe I didn't know. We talked almost every day.

She opened her laptop, which was sitting in front of her, and pushed the two letters to the side. It wasn't too late in the day to send an email, so she pulled up her account and drafted a note to Annabeth Carmichael, indicating she would be at their office at nine the next morning to discuss the Jameson Prescott letter she received. Within moments of hitting send, a reply arrived from Ms. Carmichael, thanking her for the expedient reply and letting Riley know she'd be ready to see her.

AFTER A RESTLESS NIGHT of tossing and turning, Riley pulled herself together and headed out to meet with the lawyer. With a combination of sadness and apprehension, she found herself walking in slow motion through the lobby of the large building. The spring sun cast a glaring light across the marble floor, causing her to shield her eyes for a moment while she tried to figure out where she was supposed to go.

 "Riley Maxwell?" a voice called to her.

She spun around to see a rather tall woman approach, wearing tall heels and a very big smile. "Uh, yeah?" she replied tentatively.

Shoving her hand out, the woman reached for Riley's and introduced herself. "Riley, I'm Annabeth Carmichael. One of Jameson Prescott's attorneys."

"Oh, hi." Riley shook the woman's hand and tried to collect herself. She was a New York City professional, but long gone were the days of dressing up in heels and a skirt for work. She'd been living in casual attire for years at this point, and the formality of the city corporate life was something she didn't miss.

"I figured I'd meet you in the lobby to expedite this process. It's quite imperative that we get some things handed over to you sooner rather than later." Annabeth smiled and waved for Riley to follow her to the elevator.

On the ride up, Riley asked, "What's the big hurry, exactly?"

A small chuckle escaped the lawyer. "Well, I think you better be sitting down for this. Come, we're almost there."

The elevator door opened and Riley followed her down another marble-floored hallway to a set of giant, oak double doors. Once they entered, the area transformed into a lush, corporate office space. There were no cubicles, but several large offices against the high-rise windows could be seen from the reception area, which they blew past.

Guess I don't need to check in.

"Have a seat," Annabeth said as they entered a large corner office at the edge of the space. She gestured to the large leather chair across from an equally large desk that was covered in papers and a short stack of files.

Riley sat tentatively, taking note of how large everything seemed. The chairs were huge, the desk dwarfed the lawyer on the other side, and the view out the floor-to-ceiling windows reminded her just how large New York was. She could see the Empire State Building and imagined what an amazing view that might be in the evenings as it was lit up.

"I'm sure you have some questions, but how about if I start and you can interrupt me at any time?" Annabeth's kindness wasn't so much unexpected as it was surprising for someone who seemed to be a high-level attorney. She was not only very pretty, with long blonde hair, a perfect manicure, and what was probably a thousand-dollar suit on, but she was sweet and welcoming.

"That would be great," Riley replied.

"Okay, wonderful. My assistant will be by with some coffee and refreshments shortly, but let's get started." Annabeth pulled out a folder from midway down her stack and laid it open in front of her. "I presume you read the letter from Mr. Prescott, so you are aware that he had no familial heirs to his estate."

Riley nodded.

"Mr. Prescott has asked that everything he had be left to you. This includes, but is not limited to, his home in Port Henry, his stocks, which will be transferred to you, any cash savings that he had, his vehicle, which is also located in Port Henry, and his dog." As if she could sense the need to pause, Ms. Carmichael looked up to see Riley scrunching her face.

"His dog?"

"Yes, and this was actually very important to Mr. Prescott," she replied.

"I didn't even know he had a dog." *I don't want a dog, why would he leave me a dog?*

"He did mention that to me the last time we spoke. But, this dog was very special to him, and he was quite clear in his

28

instructions that the dog was to be looked after by you specifically."

"Did he say why? I don't know anything about dogs. I've never even had a dog." Riley started to glance around the room, worried the dog might be there and she'd have to take it home to her apartment.

Annabeth giggled. "The dog is at the house in Port Henry, Ms. Maxwell. Bernard, who I believe you met the other day, is taking care of him, but Mr. Prescott wanted you to go to Port Henry as soon as possible to take ownership of the dog and of the house."

"So he told you that he wanted me to leave the city, to go to his home in Port Henry and take his *dog*?" Suddenly, she wondered if Jameson knew her at all. The city was her home, not the beach, and while they had discussed a vacation-style business meeting at the house in the Port, she certainly didn't want to move up there. "Did he expect me to live there?"

"I'm not sure what he expected you to do with the house exactly, Ms. Maxwell, but what I do know is that he'd hoped you'd consider spending the summer there, with the dog, and with the assistance of Bernard, before you make any decisions about keeping any of it. He was your only client, am I correct?" she asked, changing the subject.

"Umm, yeah. He was. He paid me in advance basically so that I'd be on retainer for his book project." She wondered what was to become of the project now that he was no longer there to give her stories.

"Yes, the book project," Annabeth thumbed through the papers in the folder before her. "Ah, here it is." She pointed to something Riley couldn't see. "Mr. Prescott would like you to continue the project without him."

"How am I supposed to write the memoirs of someone who is…" She trailed off.

"Mr. Prescott indicated that after a summer in the Port, you'd be able to gather the remaining information you need to complete the assignment. He said that he included information about resources in his personal letter to you."

"I see. Is there anything else?" Riley was shifting in her seat and wished she'd never made the trip to visit the lawyer's office. All of this information was overwhelming, and she had a strong desire to get back to her apartment and hide under the covers.

Annabeth leaned back in her chair and pulled open a drawer. She lifted out an envelope that appeared to be quite full and set it in front of Riley. "Ms. Maxwell, Mr. Prescott was very wealthy. I'm sure you knew that. His death was not exactly unexpected, but he had hoped the treatments in Switzerland would extend his life and that he'd be able to explain much of this to you himself. Unfortunately, that didn't happen. But, he has ensured that you are to be well taken care of, and in the interim of transferring ownership of his assets to you, I was instructed to give you this." She waved gently to the envelope. "Go ahead, open it."

Riley opened the envelope and found a stack of one-hundred-dollar bills, along with two credit cards in her name and a key. Her eyes widened and she quickly closed the envelope. "What is this?" she stuttered, completely in shock at the amount of cash before her.

"That… is ten thousand dollars. It is the exact amount that can legally be gifted without any annoying paperwork." She smiled. "The credit cards are linked to accounts that were opened in your name some time ago in case of an emergency or the situation we find before us. Mr. Prescott wanted you to go to the Port, he said that you knew that and were planning to go, is that correct?"

"Well, yes, that's true," she replied. "We didn't have any

set plans though. It was something we talked about the last time–" Riley stopped mid-sentence, realizing that was the last conversation she'd had with her friend.

"I know this all seems overwhelming, but my advice would be to get yourself a train ticket this afternoon and go to Port Henry. Bernard knew Mr. Prescott better than I did, and he can speak to his personal wishes far greater than I can. I don't know why he was so concerned that you take care of this dog, but maybe meet the dog. Spend a little time in your dear friend's home, which is now yours, and relax. Learn about him. You might be surprised and find that this is exactly what you need."

Riley considered what the lawyer said, and nodded. "This was truly important to him?"

Annabeth nodded. "I can say with absolute certainty that it was."

"Okay then."

LATER THAT AFTERNOON, after going over a few more legal issues and signing some papers she wasn't entirely sure about, Riley found herself on the train to the Port. She'd visited once as a teenager but had never been to one of the mansions there. Deciding to call it an adventure of sorts, and in effect, honoring her friend, she went to Port Henry, hoping this dog wasn't going to get too attached to her.

CHAPTER 5

DONOVAN

The news of the passing of Jameson Prescott hit Donovan harder than he expected it to. When he got back to the office after walking the dogs, he told Toni some of what he'd found out. After they reminisced about Scrappy and how funny Jameson had been when he got his monstrous new puppy, Donovan worried who the beneficiary of the estate was.

"I hope they like dogs," he said.

"You mean, you hope they like giant dogs that walk around like a bull in a china shop," Toni said, laughing.

Scrappy was by far, the biggest, clumsiest dog on the planet. At least that's what Donovan thought. Every time Jameson brought him in for his shots or a check-up, that dog would break at least one thing, usually more, with his tail flinging around like a lion tamer's whip. He still wasn't full-grown and at about ninety pounds the last time he was in the office, Donovan imagined he'd be bigger already.

"Do you think he knew how big that dog would get?" he asked her.

"I don't think he cared. He was looking for a companion that wouldn't turn into another ex-wife, if you ask me."

"That's a good point. You know he didn't have any family?"

"I did know that. He was a nice man. What do you think will happen to his house, and to Scrappy? Is Bernard going to keep him?" she asked.

"Bernard said that Prescott had a beneficiary and they'd be there soon," he replied.

"Interesting. Did he say who it was?"

"He did not. I guess we'll find out soon enough in this small town. I'm sure the vultures are out, hoping his property goes on the market soon."

"Well, whoever it is should keep that house. It's an excellent investment," she replied.

Donovan laughed. "Look at you, Miss 'it's a good investment.' You've turned into quite the mogul yourself."

"Fuck off, Donovan. It's not news that the property value here goes up year over year. Just because I got a payout after divorcing a lecherous asshole doesn't make me any less wealthy than the other trophy wives in this town. Only difference is, I don't have to give a blow job to my annoying husband for a new purse. I can just go buy one for myself now." She pursed her lips and put her hand on her hip dramatically, adding flair to her point.

"Touché, milady." Donovan mock saluted her and chuckled. "I didn't mean to imply you didn't deserve what you have," he offered apologetically.

"I know. I'm just telling you how it is around here.

Sometimes I think you forget that I'm a townie just like you. Just because I have some money now doesn't mean I'm an idiot. I got what I deserved in that divorce, especially after the bullshit I had to deal with in that family. They were lucky I took a payout instead of making them pay me a stipend for the rest of my life. I just didn't want to deal with them anymore, and even still, I have to see that piece of shit with his new lady around town."

"I haven't seen them, but I heard he was engaged again. I'm sorry."

"Don't be sorry for me, be sorry for that fool. She surely has stars in her eyes, and I'm certain she has no idea what sort of life she's signed up for. But, maybe she doesn't care. There's a lot of women in this town who only care about being taken care of, and are perfectly happy to keep their mouths shut and fuck when they're asked to, for payment in jewelry, clothes, and an oppulent life. I'm just not one of them. I'm no prostitute."

"You really think these wives are prostituting themselves to their husbands? Isn't that a little bitter?" Donovan tread carefully, but he was genuinely curious what Toni's opinion on the topic was, especially since she'd been on the other side.

"Okay, prostitution is a strong word. But they're robots. They do what they're told, and in return, they get stuff. Whatever superficial stuff filling the void of having no opinions or feelings causes. Eventually, some of them get tired of that Stepford life, but from what I saw, that's a true life goal for others. They feel honored to be put in that position. I was always too much for my ex. The things he loved about me in the beginning, the things that make me who I am... my sass, my opinions, my wild attitude... they all drew him to me until it was time to settle down, then he wanted to change me. At first, I thought it was part of growing up, but then I realized that it was to fit me into a cookie-cutter life that was dictated down for generations. Anyway, I'm not an idiot, and I got away and made myself a deal that sets me up for success. So, fuck off."

"Fair enough," Donovan replied, grinning back at her.

THE REST OF THE AFTERNOON, he thought about what Toni had said, that a lot of the women in the Port weren't truly happy, they were simply filling a role. It made him think over some of the summer choices he'd made the last few years as the playboy veterinarian, and he wasn't sure he liked being the guy that gave them what they wanted in the bedroom and nowhere else. Sure, it was fun at the moment, and everyone involved was always a consenting adult, but had he put himself in the category of men who weren't valued either? *Had I become the town gigolo?*

At the end of the workday, Donovan was still unsettled, so he hit up his best friend Gavin Fraser for a drink. The two had spent many a summer pursuing the ladies of the Port, offering their services as it were, and with summer approaching, what better time to get his head back in the game of fun than a few drinks with his buddy.

AFTER A SHOWER and an internal pep talk, Donovan met up with Gavin at their usual watering hole, the Rusty Scupper. One of the oldest bar and restaurants in the area, it was a place both the townies and tourists frequented, with amazing food, reasonably priced drinks, and a summery, nautical vibe that appealed to the area.

"We eating, or just drinking tonight?" Gavin said, patting his friend on the back.

"Just drinking, I think," Donovan replied, not entirely sure. He was happy to see his old friend. Gavin was a real estate agent in the Port, and a busy one at that. Houses and properties were constantly changing hands, being foreclosed on, or inherited, for that matter. "How's business?"

"Better than ever!" he exclaimed. "There are six new properties on the market, and I've already got offers pouring in. Rock stars, actresses, and even a famous TV chef are all bidding on one of them. It's gonna be a good summer." He rubbed his palms together. "How are the pets of the rich and famous?"

"I don't think any of my patients are particularly famous." Donovan laughed. "They are rich though."

"Fair enough. How's that hot tech of yours? Toni, is it?"

"She's good, and she's off-limits," Donovan replied sternly. Friends or not, he wasn't about to let Gavin try to sweet talk Toni into some kind of summer fling. Not that she'd accept—he was pretty sure Toni had her own game in town, but she was hush-hush about it.

"Okay, okay." Gavin put his hands up in surrender. "No hot assistants. Got it."

"Thank you." Donovan rolled his eyes.

"So, what's new? Anything else besides work?" Gavin had a gleam in his eye as he scanned the room. "Either the women are getting younger, or the plastic surgeons are getting better. We gonna be each other's wingman this season again or what?"

As despicable a thing as it was to say, he was right. Donovan glanced around the room as well, and the beautiful people were showing up in full force. For a mid-week night, the bar was full, and the restaurant had a waitlist already. There were a lot of familiar faces, although several of them looked like they'd had a freshening up in the offseason. "Uh, yeah. I'd say it's business as usual. That's why we work so hard all winter, right?" Donovan wasn't sure he meant what he said, but he could sense it wasn't the time to have a conflict of morals discussion with his friend.

The bar was situated near the front door and when *she* walked in, it was quite the ruckus. With a giant suitcase on wheels, a small purse strapped across her body, and a laptop bag, the woman slung the door open wildly, causing some of the long dark hair that had been piled on top of her head to fall down past her shoulders. It seemed as though she wasn't quite sure where she was as she looked around the room with a raised eyebrow.

She dragged her suitcase over to the bar and plopped down two seats away from Donovan and Gavin, who watched her silently. When the bartender came over and asked what she wanted, her reply was even more surprising.

"I'm gonna need a shot of tequila. You know what? Make that two," she said as she rested both hands on top of the bar and took a deep breath.

Donovan couldn't take his eyes off her. Dressed in cutoff jean shorts, a ripped sweatshirt, and canvas shoes, she wasn't like anyone else he'd seen of late, and she definitely wasn't a townie. Before he could say anything, Gavin whispered, "Dibs!" excitedly.

"Hold on just a second. She just walked in," Donovan replied.

"Since when did that matter?" Gavin shrugged his shoulders and blew his friend off, approaching the new girl.

"Can I buy you a drink?" he asked her in his smarmy way. Donovan had no reason to be jealous, he didn't even know the girl, but he knew he didn't want Gavin's grubby hands on her.

"I already have two, thanks." She held up her shot glass up to show him before taking it down like a college kid on spring break.

"You're new to Port Henry, aren't you?" he asked her, completely unfazed by her disinterest.

"What gave it away? The clothes from the mall?" she replied sarcastically. Her sunglasses were tucked into her hair on top of her head, and her body language definitely indicated she wanted him to go away. She'd turned herself on the bar stool to face away from him without being too blunt, but Gavin wasn't one for taking hints.

"So what brings you to the Port? You here for the summer?" Innuendo dripped from his mouth as Gavin leaned in closer to her. Donovan watched the scene unfold, shaking his head and sipping his beer.

The young woman, whose pale face and pink lips were in stark contrast, shut her eyes and sighed deeply. She picked up her other shot glass, downed the amber liquid like a champ, and locked eyes with Gavin. "What's your name?" she asked him.

Grinning, he replied, "I'm Gavin. Gavin Fraser." He put his hand out for her to take, but she didn't.

"Listen, Gavin Fraser." She sneered down at his outstretched hand while Gavin continued to grin, blissfully unaware she was about to crush his confident swagger, something Donovan saw coming from their first interaction. "I'm sure that your pretty boy, charming personality works on the local gals in the offseason and, hell, maybe it even works on the rich tourists all summer. But you won't be adding this"—she waved her hands down the front of herself—"to your body count. I don't have any interest in a fuck in the bathroom or a one-night stand, or even a summer fling with some wannabe rich boy looking to whet his whistle for the season. You got me?"

Donovan choked on his beer audibly, garnering her attention. "Don't you bother either. You two are easy to spot a mile away, with your good looks and nice clothes. I'm not buying what you're selling."

"Who me?" Donovan asked defensively. "I didn't say anything!"

"You didn't have to. I can tell exactly what you two are up to, perched at the bar, making your plans for the summer like horny vultures. It's written all over your faces." She pointed her index and ring fingers at both of them with judgment. Hopping off the bar, she dug some cash out of her pocket and dropped a fifty-dollar bill on the bar before dragging her giant suitcase behind her, leaving as dramatically as she had arrived.

Donovan grinned like he'd just watched his favorite team win the World Series.

I think I'm in love.

CHAPTER 6

RILEY

I f that's what Port Henry had to offer in the way of local hospitality, I won't be staying long. What a couple of creeps.

Riley stormed back out of the Rusty Scupper, the taste of tequila still swirling in her mouth. Thinking that was probably not the best of ideas, she pulled a bottle of water out of her laptop bag and took a long drink. Annabeth had offered to make travel arrangements—well, she'd offered to have her assistant make travel arrangements for her—but her pride made her say she'd take care of it herself. The truth was, the lawyer's office, and the overflow of information and building emotions, made her feel trapped, so she took her envelope of cash and went back home as quickly as she could to pack and get herself to the Port.

By car, and with no traffic, it was only a ninety-minute ride, but Riley didn't drive. She knew how to, but had no use for a car in the city and didn't have one, so she opted to take the train. Once she arrived in the Port, she wasn't quite ready to see Bernard again, or to meet this dog that was so damn important to Jameson. *Why would he think I'd want that responsibility?* She groaned to herself.

Now, she was stranded outside the restaurant and needed to get a ride to the house. She looked at the map on her phone to see if it was within walking distance, and it appeared to be just a mere half a mile away. Twenty blocks was about a mile in the city, so she decided walking the half-mile would be easy enough, even if she was dragging a suitcase behind her.

After she'd been walking for around ten minutes, a black SUV pulled up next to her and rolled down its tinted window. *Oh God, what now?*

"Need a lift?" the stranger called out.

Neither stopping nor making eye contact, she shouted, "No thanks. I'm good."

The SUV continued to drive at a snail's pace alongside her, giving her the distinct sense someone needed a proper New York City blow off. *What is it with this town?*

"Listen, I'm sorry about my friend. You're obviously new in town, he didn't mean to be as creepy as he was."

Oh great, the other hot guy from the bar is now following me. This is how you end up on Dateline *after they find your body in the woods.*

"And you don't think following me down the street in your tricked out Escalade is creepy at all?" she snarled back and stared at him through her sunglasses.

He gave her a half-smile and nodded. "Fair enough. I can assure you I'm not a creep. My name is Donovan. Donovan Hunter."

Riley's patience was nearing its breaking point with these strangers, and introducing himself on the side of the road from his fancy car didn't make him any less annoying or strange. "Well, Donovan Hunter, I do not need a ride. Thank you for your offer."

She turned away and got back to her walk. A quick glance at her phone revealed she was only a block or two away from her destination and while she was getting hot in the sun, she was damned sure not taking a ride from a stranger. She could make it a couple more blocks on pride alone.

He continued to keep pace with her for another moment before asking again, "Are you sure I can't give you a lift? That suitcase looks heavy." His tone was kind and he was right, the suitcase was heavy. Riley had thrown a rather random assortment of clothing and things she thought she might need into it with little thought of how much it would weigh.

"I'm sure. But thanks again. I'm almost where I need to be."

"You're not gonna tell me where that is, are you?" He laughed, seeming to enjoy the banter they were having on the side of the road.

"No, I'm not."

"Well, I hope to see you again..." He paused, she presumed to imply he wanted her name.

"Uh, okay, Donovan Hunter. See ya around." She half-waved, continuing to avoid eye contact as she moved toward her destination.

He rolled the window up and did a U-turn in the middle of the street, heading in the opposite direction. Riley shook her head and muttered to herself, *What the fuck have I gotten myself into?*

Lugging the suitcase along the side of the road turned out to be a bit more arduous than Riley expected and she'd wished she called for a taxi or a rideshare by the time

Donovan had offered her a ride. She'd even considered accepting his offer briefly, but thought better of it when her city stranger meter kicked in. *It probably would have been perfectly fine, but I'm not here to make friends.*

Finally, she arrived at Jameson's address. The house was exactly what she had expected. From the exterior, you could see floor-to-ceiling windows and a giant chandelier in the foyer. It was painted a pale blue befitting the landscape, and had stark white shutters. It was pristine but also gave the vibe that it was comfortable inside. As she ventured down the last stretch of driveway, the door flew open and before she knew what hit her, a massive dog jumped up on her and was licking her face.

"Oh my God!" she cried out as she tumbled to the ground. The dog must have thought she was playing because he stood on top of her, practically crushing her ribs while continuing to bathe her in spit. As she tried to cover her face to make him stop, she heard Bernard's voice.

"Scrappy! That's enough!" he bellowed.

The dog removed himself from her chest and sat next to her, tail wagging at a record-setting pace while Riley sat up, reeling from the shock.

"What the hell?" she grumbled.

"Ms. Maxwell, you're here," Bernard said with some surprise. "I wasn't expecting you. I could have picked you up."

Lifting herself off the ground, Riley glared at the dog. "I guess this is my new dog, huh?" she said, brushing the dirt off.

Bernard laughed. "Why yes, this is Scrappy. He's very excited to meet you."

Well, that makes one of us.

"Uh-huh. Is that what that is?" she replied sarcastically.

Bernard stepped closer and picked up Riley's suitcase. "Let me get that for you."

"Thanks," she said.

"Follow me and we'll get you settled," Bernard offered as he took her bag into the house.

Walking behind him, she glared at the dog again, who appeared to be doing everything in his power to sit still, awaiting permission to move.

"Scrappy, get in the house," Bernard addressed the monstrous beast, who hopped up and pranced into the house ahead of them. For such a huge dog, he was light on his feet when he wasn't toppling you over.

"Scrappy?" Riley asked, a hint of derision still in her voice.

Bernard laughed again. "Mr. Prescott had a sense of humor... as you know. And, I mean Scrappy was *kinda* small as a puppy. Although, he's still technically a puppy."

"You mean to tell me that brute isn't full-grown?" Riley couldn't believe the dog still had growing to do.

"No, not yet. He still has about another twenty pounds or so he'll probably put on. His energy level is all puppy though." Bernard placed Riley's suitcase at the bottom of a beautiful staircase that spiraled halfway to the second floor before straightening out alongside the wall the rest of the way up. "Your room is upstairs, but I thought you might want some refreshment?"

"That would be great," Riley replied haphazardly as she gazed about the parts of the house she could see. As she'd expected from the outside, the inside was gorgeous. She could see couches across the back end of the house where more floor-to-ceiling glass looked out over the water.

"Why don't you have a seat out on the back porch and I'll grab us a drink. I'm sure you have a lot of questions you'd like answered." He waved his hand toward the area she'd been peering at from afar. "I would have made arrangements to come and get you," he said again.

"That's okay, Bernard. I needed to spend a little time, walking and acclimating."

"Understood." He walked off to the right where the kitchen seemed to be, and Riley followed him until she reached the back door, which was almost entirely glass.

Scrappy had settled himself onto a large dog bed until she opened the back door, at which point he trotted over to her. "Oh, you want to go outside too?"

Before she let him follow her, she looked out to the deck to see if it was safe. Beautiful teak lounge chairs were placed around the area in what created little seating areas for small groups of people to congregate. She spotted a dog bed next to one of the chaise lounges, indicating to her that Scrappy could join her outside.

"Don't run away or jump on me again, got it?" she said to him before letting him lead the way to his favorite spot, which turned out to be the chaise lounge *next* to the dog bed, not the dog bed itself. "Whatever, just be chill." Riley rolled her eyes at the dog, who had stretched himself out, so much so that his back and front paws were both hanging off the edges. He let out a very loud sigh and stared at her.

"Dude, I don't know what to tell you. I don't know what I'm doing here," she explained to him.

"Well, this is your home," Bernard interrupted her conversation with Scrappy, setting down two lemonades and a bottle of vodka on the matching table between them. "If you want it to be." He handed her a glass. "I thought you might want a real drink after the long trip, and what with the craziness of the day I assume you have had."

"You assume correctly, Bernard." She smiled as she

replied before taking a long sip of the cool lemonade. *No need to mention the shots of tequila I had before.*

Bernard settled himself in the chair across from her and glanced over at the dog. "Damn dog loves to lay on the furniture. Thinks he's a human."

"So, about this dog…" Riley decided to use that as her segway to not keeping the dog.

"He's a good dog, but he's huge. And clumsy." Bernard chuckled. "Mr. Prescott put all the glass away when Scrappy here was a puppy because that tail of his kept knocking everything onto the floor."

"Why did Jameson leave me a dog? He knows—knew—that I lived in the city. How the hell would I be able to take this guy into an apartment?" She cut right to the chase.

"Mr. Prescott hoped that you would spend the summer here at the shore."

"Did you know that he was dying?" Riley asked bluntly.

"I knew that he was very sick. But he was doing everything in his power to get well. Unfortunately, it was just simply his time."

"So you knew what was in the letter he gave me?" she asked.

"I did not. That was a personal letter, for you."

"Why did he leave everything to me and not you? He only knew me for like, eighteen months, tops."

"Mr. Prescott has taken care of me and ensured that I want for nothing. But the house, and the assets, they were for you. I have all that I need. I will live here as long as you want me to, and I'll continue my duties here so long as you see fit. Should you decide you no longer wish to have my services, I will move on."

He seemed cold and distant in his reply, and Riley didn't mean to upset or hurt Bernard's feelings. She knew she needed to tone her city style down a bit and be the Riley who was friends with Jameson. "You will stay as long as you want to, Bernard. But you don't have to wait on me. I can take care of myself."

Bernard grinned and lifted his glass of lemonade to toast. "Welcome to Port Henry, Riley."

She clinked his glass with hers, and leaned back in the comfy chair, taking in the evening breeze. *Maybe a vacation would do me some good. What better way to figure out what's next than in a mansion you've just inherited?*

CHAPTER 7

DONOVAN

he was right, it was totally creeper of me to follow her down the road. Donovan felt like a jackass. At the moment, it seemed like the only way to show her he wasn't like Gavin. Unsure why he suddenly felt the need to separate who he was as a person from his best friend, he chalked it up to a weird day and headed home. He was ready to spend the rest of the night on the couch.

He watched some television and played with the dogs but when it was time to go to bed, he couldn't stop thinking of the stranger dragging her suitcase down the road. Not only was she beautiful, and her features striking, but she was also hilarious. When she told Gavin off, calling him out as a letch, he couldn't contain his laughter. Nobody had made him laugh that hard as long as he could recall, except maybe Toni.

Donovan lay in bed, wondering if he'd see her again. She was walking toward the residential side of town, so she had to be on her way to someone's house. Tapping his temple, he ran through the residents he knew in that area but he wasn't aware of anyone who would start having summer guests quite that early in the season. Sighing, he gave up to get some sleep. After all, he still had to work in the morning.

THE NEXT DAY at the office was extraordinarily busy. Matthew Maloni's turtle wasn't eating, Mrs. Chadwick's two chihuahuas needed their teeth cleaned, which required sedation—for her and the dogs—and little Tommy Grimaldi had found a sick baby bird that needed medical attention, as it appeared to have fallen from its nest.

While attempting to bottle feed the baby bird, which looked like a little robin, a large crash came from outside the exam room where he was delicately holding the chick. Thankfully, he had a steady hand and didn't crush the tiny thing, but the dog barking loudly and the crash meant they had another patient on their hands. Donovan placed the little bird in an incubator, checked to make sure the temperature was set, and made his way to the waiting room.

He hadn't gotten halfway down the hall when he was nearly tackled by a giant dog whose leash was swinging behind him. Instantly, he knew who it was. "Scrappy!" he said, taking the dog's giant paws off his shoulders. Donovan was six foot three and Scrappy had no problem at all stretching out to his height to hug him like a human, and he wasn't even fully grown. "What are you doing here, boy?"

"I'm so sorry, I tried to hold on, but…" The woman from yesterday rounded the corner, apparently looking for Scrappy. "Oh," she said when she recognized Donovan.

"Well, hello there, Miss…?" Donovan grinned, feeling as

though he'd won the "now you have to tell me your name" game.

"Maxwell. Riley Maxwell," she replied, pursing her lips in defeat. "This is—"

"This is Scrappy," Donovan cut her off. "I know who he is, but why do you have him?" Then, it dawned on him. Riley was Jameson Prescott's beneficiary. Why else would she have Scrappy? While he was still sorting out the connection mentally, Riley interrupted his thoughts.

"Um, so you're the vet?" she asked.

"Oh, yes. I am," he replied. "Is something wrong with Scrappy?" He glanced down at the dog, who was calmly leaning against his leg, tail wagging.

"I'm not sure," she replied.

Confused, Donovan asked, "What are you doing here?"

"Well, Scrappy here decided to eat a pair of my shoes. He also ate a tree."

"He ate a tree?"

"A whole fucking tree, outside. I let him out to do his business this morning after he had eaten my shoes, and then, before I knew what was happening, he'd ripped a sapling, I mean, I guess it was bigger than a sapling, he didn't eat an oak tree or anything, but he ate a small tree and I don't know a lot about dogs, but I'm pretty sure they're not supposed to eat shoes and trees." Riley rambled everything out without taking a breath, and when she finished, she sighed. "So, is he gonna be okay?"

Trying to hold back a laugh, Donovan pointed to the door across the hall between them. "Take Scrappy in there, and I'll be in shortly to check him out." Once Riley was in the exam room with the door shut, he chuckled out loud and swung by Toni's desk. "Did you get all that?" he asked.

Toni grinned. "I'm guessing she's the one who inherited

the dog?"

"Seems so. Did you get the story?"

"I got enough to know she doesn't know anything about dogs like Scrappy. She's got her hands full with that one. Sorry I didn't stop him. My hands were full, and I figured he wouldn't get far."

"No problem. I'm gonna check him out, just to make sure he doesn't have any obstructions or anything. Can you check on Bartholomew?"

Toni had a puzzled look on her face, then she realized, "Oh, the turtle. Yep, I'll go see if he's eaten yet so he can go home." The turtle had a fractured leg, but also hadn't been eating. Once they saw he'd consumed some food, they'd let him go home. She rose from her chair and headed to the back where Bartholomew's cage was set up while Donovan made his way back to the exam room.

"Hi there, sorry about that. It's been a very busy day. Let's take a look at Scrappy here." Donovan ran his hands over and palpated the dog's abdomen, feeling for anything that might be cause for concern. It was fairly common for a dog of his breed to eat some unusual stuff, and they typically grew out of that phase with age and good training. "So, he ate the shoes and the...tree. Did he eat any of his actual food?"

"Yes, all of it."

"Before or after he went outside?" Donovan placed his stethoscope in his ears and listened to Scrappy's belly, as well as his heart. There were no unusual sounds and Scrappy was acting perfectly normal... well, for Scrappy at least.

"Before. Is he going to be okay?" Riley asked, her voice trembling a bit.

Donovan placed his stethoscope around his neck and patted Scrappy on the head, then scratched his ears. "He's probably going to take an enormous dump this afternoon, but otherwise, he's just fine. Make sure he drinks a lot of water, and he should skip his normal dinner tonight."

Riley sighed deeply. "Thank you so much."

"It's not a problem, Miss Maxwell," he replied formally.

"You can call me Riley. And, I'm sorry I was so rude to you yesterday. It's been a really weird week for me." Her blue eyes glazed over a bit, as if she might cry, melting Donovan's snarky demeanor.

"So, you inherited Scrappy here?" Donovan was still petting the dog, who was now leaning into him, encouraging more rubs all over his giant head.

"I did. And in case you hadn't noticed, I don't know a whole lot about dogs." She half-smiled and shrugged her shoulders. "But, I'm trying. I've only had him since yesterday, and he's kind of a menace, to be honest."

Donovan let out a hearty laugh. "Well, Great Danes can be a handful, but they're also very loyal and loving. Once you get to know each other, he'll be your best friend."

"I'm not sure I'm going to keep him," she admitted.

"Why wouldn't you keep him?" Donovan asked, rather surprised.

"I live in the city, and I don't think a city apartment is a very good place for a giant dog, do you?"

"Aren't you staying in Jameson's place now?" he asked.

"I am, but that's temporary until I figure out what I'm going to do with the house and everything."

"Would you sell it?" Donovan was shocked she wouldn't want to keep the house; it was stunning and extremely valuable.

Riley started shifting her weight back and forth, and looked uncomfortable. "I don't know what I'm going to do. I haven't figured anything out yet. I just got here," she replied, some defense in her tone.

"I'm sorry, I didn't mean to pry. It's none of my business. But you should stay for a bit, Port Henry is a wonderful place to spend the summer if you can. Plus, the beach is good for thinking," he said, offering her a warm smile.

"Thank you, Doctor. I'm so sorry I took up so much of your time with a dog that eats shoes. Come on, Scrappy," she said to the dog. Scrappy looked up at her, getting excited again. His tail began to wag feverishly again, and his front paws came up and down off the floor, just enough to let them know he wanted to jump on her, but was restraining himself.

"Do you need a ride home?" Donovan asked, not even thinking before he spoke.

Riley laughed. "You must really want to drive me around, eh, Doctor?"

"You can call me Donovan," he replied, feeling his own face flush a bit with embarrassment.

"Well, Donovan, I drove one of Jameson's cars here. Scrappy is actually a very good passenger, aren't you, boy?" He let out a low, quiet bark as if to reply that he was indeed a good passenger, and a good boy.

"Can't blame a guy for trying." Donovan laughed. "It was nice to meet you again." He extended his hand, which she politely took.

"Thank you again for your help, and for the numerous offers of a ride." She gave him a sweet smile and giggled quietly. "Come on, Scrappy, I'm sure the doctor has actual sick patients to see. Let's go."

Scrappy trotted over to Riley, who grabbed his leash. She let herself out of the exam room, but not before glancing back at Donovan, where she smiled again before she left. The door shut behind her and Donovan ran his hands through his thick, dark hair.

Oh man, she's adorable.

CHAPTER 8

RILEY

"Thanks for embarrassing me, dog," Riley muttered to him as she buckled his seat belt. Scrappy was big enough to sit in the front seat and be belted in like a regular person. She couldn't believe he was only going to get bigger. *He has to be almost as big as me.*

After making sure the dog was snug in his seat, Riley sat down in the driver's seat and sighed before turning the car on. She drove so little, she had to psyche herself up to do it. Some people truly enjoyed driving, and going on road trips, but Riley preferred walking and taking public transit. When she left to take Scrappy to the vet, Bernard had offered to drive them, but she didn't want him feeling like he was her manservant. His doting was stifling for someone who typically spent a tremendous amount of time alone.

"Okay, let's do this," she said.

Scrappy let out a reciprocal "woof" in reply.

Riley chuckled and drove them back to Jameson's house, where she'd made afternoon plans to go through some of his things.

LATER THAT DAY, Riley sat in Jameson's office, rummaging through his desk drawers. Bernard had asked if she needed any help, but she explained she was just trying to figure out what needed to be kept and what should be filed away. The truth was, she was snooping, and while Bernard may have known what she was up to, he wasn't interfering and left her to it, which was precisely what she wanted. Scrappy, meanwhile, had parked himself on the chaise lounge under the window. A bit of sun shone through, and he stretched his gigantic body out like a human stretches in the mornings. With his toes hanging off the edge, he fell dead asleep on his back.

Riley began by casually looking through Jameson's book collection. On a giant wall behind the desk from about midway up, all the way to the ceiling, were built-in bookshelves. She ran her hand across the spines gently, wondering if Jameson had read all of them. They were organized by theme and genre mostly, with the classics all together. Copies of Shakespeare, Bronte, and Fitzgerald sat side by side, and then there were business and reference books, all neatly organized as well. He even had a set of philosophy books, the likes of which she hadn't seen since college. Most of the books were hardbacks, although there were a few paperbacks scattered amongst the others.

Once she'd perused the shelves, she decided to settle in and go through his desk. *Technically, everything here belongs to me, so it's not really snooping,* she said to herself as she opened the first drawer and peeked inside. *Nothing interesting.* Just some pens and blank paper, along with random office supplies, like paper clips and staples.

The second drawer she tried to open was locked. She yanked on it harder, but it wouldn't budge. Riley searched through the little boxes along the edge of the desk to see if any of them held the key to the drawer, but she found nothing but push pins, loose change, and more paper clips. A locked drawer tended to hold secrets and she decided if she couldn't find the key, she'd break into it anyway.

Riley glanced around to make sure Bernard was out of earshot, and she took a large, metal letter opener from the other drawer and jammed it into the space between the locked drawer and the desk itself. She managed to damage the wood around the lock just enough to pry it open. "Yes!" she congratulated herself quietly.

She slid the drawer open slowly, then pulled out a folder of photographs. At first, she didn't recognize anyone in them, but soon she realized there was a picture of someone she knew better than anyone.

A knock on the door startled her and she shoved the photographs back in the drawer. "Yes?" she called out, trying not to sound as shaken as she was.

"Miss Maxwell, you have a visitor." It was Bernard, but she wasn't expecting any visitors. In fact, she wasn't even sure she'd told Colette what was happening, or that she was in Port Henry. Making a mental note to call her best friend, she stood up from the desk.

"Who is it?" she asked.

"It's me, uh, Donovan." The doctor poked his head around the corner apprehensively.

"Oh, hi, Dr. Hunter… Donovan," Riley replied, surprised to see him.

Scrappy peeled himself from his perch, stretched into downward dog, then trotted over to Donovan for head scratches.

"I just wanted to come by and see how you and Scrappy here were doing," he said, a bit of apprehension in his voice.

Riley wanted to take the pictures, but didn't want anyone to see them, so she had no choice but to leave them in the now unlocked drawer. "That was very kind of you, but we're both doing fine. As you can see, the king of the castle here is as spry as ever." She nodded in the direction of the dog, who she was certain smirked at her. *Can dogs smirk?*

"It certainly looks like he's just fine." Donovan shifted nervously in place, continuing to rub Scrappy's head, much to the dog's delight.

"Um, would you like a drink or something?" She wasn't quite sure of the protocol for guests who stopped by, since she wasn't used to having any. Drinks seemed appropriate.

"Sure, that would be great," he replied. Donovan appeared to relax at the offer of drinks, and he followed Riley out to the patio. The sun had begun to set and the temperature was a cool seventy, perfect for sitting outside.

"Is this okay?" she asked.

"Yeah, this is great."

"Okay, I"ll be right back. Do you like vodka or beer? I know that we have both of those. I'm not really sure what else there is."

"A beer would be nice," he replied.

Riley walked off to the kitchen and grabbed two beers from the fridge. Bernard was sitting at the bar, reading a novel. "I would have brought those out for you, Riley."

"You enjoy your book, Bernard. You deserve to relax too. If Dr. Hunter decides to stay a while, maybe you could help me put some snacks together though? I'm not very good in the kitchen," she asked.

"It would be my pleasure." The old man smiled. Riley truly didn't want him waiting on her hand and foot, but it seemed to trouble him she hadn't given him anything to do, so snacks was a win-win.

"Okay, awesome. Maybe in like, an hour?"

"I'm on it," he replied.

Riley took the two beers out to the patio and handed one to Donovan. "None of these are my groceries, so I'm still kind of figuring out what we have here. Hope this is okay."

"It's perfect, thank you."

Scrappy had settled himself next to Donovan, clearly realizing that was where the most attention would come from.

"So, did you really stop by just to see how this big lug of a dog was doing?" Dancing around a point was never her forte, and she hadn't planned on starting now. Might as well find out what this guy's agenda was out of the gate.

"I'm just being neighborly, and a good veterinarian," he said with a grin. "And, yes, I wanted to come see you as well. I wanted to apologize for being so nosy about what your intentions were. I never even told you how sorry I was for your loss. You and Jameson must have been quite close for him to leave you with"—Donovan gestured his hands around the space—"all this?"

Riley eyed Donovan from across the table that separated them. She didn't have anyone to confide in, but she also didn't know this guy at all. He was friends with that turd Gavin though. Even still, her half-smile was unavoidable. "Jameson and I knew each other and worked very closely together for the last eighteen months or so."

"So, you were work colleagues?" Donovan asked.

"Sort of."

Donovan waited for her to say more and when she didn't offer, he asked, "When was the last time you saw him?"

"It was about a year ago. I did work for him from the city." Riley wasn't ready to discuss Jameson's memoirs. They seemed too personal and while she knew he wanted them finished, she hadn't come to terms with it just yet.

"Oh, really? What do you do?"

"I'm a writer, mostly. I was writing some things for him," she offered, hoping he wouldn't ask for more detail.

"Jameson is… was, a particular man. You must be quite good at it."

The flattery was not lost on her, and Riley blushed a little. "I'm not bad." She grinned. "So, Doctor, why don't you tell me about this town of yours. What am I missing out on?"

Donovan chuckled. "Well, the summer is just beginning here in the Port. The people watching is to die for, and there's usually quite a few celebrities walking about. I'd say in about two weeks, people will start rolling in for the summer."

"I'd heard that, but I've never been here before. Except one time, as a kid." She glanced out to the water. "Would you like to go for a walk? I haven't been down to the water since I arrived yesterday, and I'd like to."

"Sure, that would be great." Donovan set his bottle down on the table and stood up, to Scrappy's dismay. His giant head had been resting on Donovan's lap.

"Do you know if I can take Scrappy out there without a leash? Will he run away?" she asked him.

"He won't run away, and his breed isn't particularly aggressive, so he should be fine."

"Come on, dog, let's go!"

Scrappy realized where they were going, and took off in a

canter ahead of Donovan and Riley as they made their way down the path to the beach. Riley wanted to get away from the house, and out of range from Bernard, so she could ask Donovan what he might know about Jameson and the secrets kept locked inside that house.

CHAPTER 9

DONOVAN

Riley and Donovan walked along the water for a bit, talking idly about Port Henry. Mostly, Donovan told her about some of his favorite things about living there, least of which was being by the water.

"I feel like it has a calming effect. It can get a little wild out here with the fancy parties and whatnot, but out here on the beach, it's different. The water soothes the soul, I think," Donovan said wistfully before realizing how silly he must sound. "I just mean… everyone seems to chill out a little more on the beach, if that makes sense." He stopped himself before he said anything else too ridiculous.

Riley giggled and agreed, nodding. "I do think there's some peace in listening to the waves. I opened my window last night so I could hear them crashing on the beach in the distance. It helped me fall asleep in a new bed, that's for sure."

"Let's sit a while," Donovan suggested.

"Right here?" Riley glanced around. There were no chairs or anything to sit on.

"Yep, right here. The sun is setting now. Let's just chill out and watch," he said, plopping down in the sand, then patted the spot next to him. "Give me your shoes." They'd been walking shoeless for some time, carrying them. Donovan took the sandals from her and put them in a small pile with his canvas loafers.

"This dog is crazy," Riley said. Scrappy was prancing around in the sand, stopping every once in a while to chase a wave out, then run from the next one that rolled ashore.

"He's still a puppy. He's surprisingly energetic for his breed, I'll give you that," Donovan said, chuckling. "Theoretically, he'll calm down. But I'll be honest. With that one, who knows?"

They both laughed and watched the dog run around a bit more before he settled himself in the sand at their feet. Watching the sun set, they sat quietly for a while, enjoying the breeze and the fresh air.

"Have you given any more thought to spending the summer here? I think you'd really like it." Donovan broke the silence that had fallen.

Riley continued to look out over the water, which became harder to see as the daylight began to disappear. "I don't have to go back right away, and I think there are some things I need to figure out about Jameson."

"What do you mean?" Donovan asked.

"I thought that I knew him well, but I'm beginning to think the Jameson Prescott that I knew—the one who was my friend—was someone else altogether."

"That sounds ominous." Donovan chuckled lightly.

"I really don't know what to do with Scrappy or this house, that's for sure. And I'm not entirely sure what else has become mine, so I need to go back to the city and figure some of that out, I think. Sooner rather than later. There's apparently paperwork that needs to be done. I don't know. This was all a huge shock."

Donovan wanted to beg her to stay. He couldn't think of any good reason why a woman he just met should listen to him, other than if it was about the dog. "Well, I know that I said Scrappy is just fine, but I do think we should keep an eye on him for at least a few days. Just to make sure he hasn't ingested anything we didn't know about. That could put him in the hospital and we wouldn't want that. So don't rush off just yet."

Riley spun toward him. "Do you think that's possible?"

Realizing he may have gone slightly overboard about the dog's condition, he decided to go with it anyway. "Well yeah, it's definitely *possible*." *Please don't strike me dead*, he said to himself, apprehensively gazing up at the sky. *Or the dog. I just like the girl and want her to stay longer.*

"Well, if that's the case, we should stay a few more days for sure," she replied. "I will probably need to find him a new home because he would be terribly unhappy in a city apartment, but until I figure that out, I have to make sure he's taken care of." She glanced over at the pup, who had not clue he might need a new home. Donovan didn't want to let that happen, and started to think of how he could entice her to stay, and to keep Scrappy.

The two sat and chatted a bit longer before making their way back to the house, a much slower, worn-out Scrappy in tow. When they arrived back at the patio, a full spread of snacks was laid out on the low table where they'd been sitting, along with two fresh bottles of beer in a small bucket of ice. Bernard had definitely hooked them up.

"You hungry?" Riley asked, gesturing toward the table and laughing at the amount of food intended to be snacks.

Donovan chuckled. "I could definitely eat."

The two sat down to eat, and Donovan wondered what about their working relationship had made Riley so important to Jameson that he would leave her everything. After they'd each had three beers, she had finally seemed to relax, but he didn't want to press her. She was vulnerable and confused about the situation, that much was evident, and he didn't want to take advantage of that. Self-discovery was leading him down a far more righteous path than previous summers, and with the arrival of the guarded newcomer, he couldn't help wanting to know her more. They continued to chat idly about the Port, and he listened as she described the things she loved in the city while watching her blue eyes light up as she spoke.

Donovan returned home that night, wishing he could have stayed longer. If Riley hadn't begun yawning, he might have. But he didn't want to overstay his welcome and he'd planted the first seed toward getting her to remain in Port Henry. When she gave him a small goodnight kiss on the cheek, he was certain she lingered there longer than she had to. He wanted to court her as if it were the olden days, when you didn't just meet a woman in a bar and take her home. Getting to know Riley was fun and Donovan couldn't recall the last time he'd had that enjoyable of an evening that didn't end in sex. As he lay in bed that night, he ran through their conversation in his head, trying to pluck out any detail that might be useful in getting her to stay.

I need to do something big, and fast. All he wanted was for her to commit to the summer so they could spend time together, get to know each other. Donovan couldn't let her leave. As crazy as it sounded, something in his bones told him she was brought here to the Port—to him—for a reason, and after the evening together, he was certain there was a part of her that felt it too.

THE NEXT MORNING, Donovan woke up with a spring in his step. He had a plan, but it was not entirely honest. Something, a gut feeling, told him he should just go with it, and fate would follow. For the first time since summer had begun to approach, he didn't look at it with apprehension. Instead, he was excited. The days of prowling for the ex-wives of the rich and famous to warm his bed were behind him. He needed someone like Riley, and the awareness of that fact was as clear as the morning on that spring day.

The Prescott house was only two miles from his own house and while his heart was sure of his next move, his head started to give him doubts. *What if she thinks I'm insane? Maybe she wasn't feeling the same connection.* His confidence waned as he pulled in the driveway, and he considered turning around and leaving, forgetting the whole plan. But when Riley opened the door and walked outside with Scrappy on a leash and their gazes met, it was do or die time.

"Oh hey, Donovan, what are you doing here?" She jogged over to his car with the dog in tow. "Did you forget something last night?"

He stepped out, forgetting the plan briefly because he was too busy taking in how pretty she was for it being so early in the morning. Her hair was once again piled up on top of her head, but she looked like she was ready to tackle the day, a look of determination spread across her face.

"Umm, sort of," he said, willing himself to go for it. "I wanted to talk to you for a minute before I went to work."

"Of course, what is it?" Her immediate and genuine interest in what he had to say sealed the deal. He needed her to stay.

Okay, say it. He ran through the lines in his head. *Riley... there's something about you I can't get out of my head. I like you. I know we just met and it's been kind of an odd set of circumstances, but I swear to you, I'm really not like Gavin, and I'd like the chance to see if there's something between us.*

"I don't have your number, so I wanted to stop by and tell you that you should bring Scrappy in so I can check him out and make sure he's not suffering any effects from all the stuff he ate yesterday." *Chickenshit.*

He looked over at the dog, who definitely tilted his head, knowing his name had been mentioned. *Don't rat me out, dog,* he said to himself.

He watched her body language change from concern to surprise. "He seems fine." She motioned toward Scrappy who continued to stare Donovan down; at least that's what he was sure was happening.

"Well, there could be underlying problems and we should monitor him closely, just to be sure," Donovan replied, knowing he was full of shit, the dog was fine.

"Okay, well, if you're sure he needs to come in, I can do that today. Is there a particular time that would be best?" Riley's concerned tone was like a punch in the gut to Donovan, and while he wanted to keep her there, he knew lying was wrong.

I just need to buy a little time to win her over, he thought. "How about if you come by at the end of the day? Keep an eye on him though, and make sure he's drinking lots of water. I should be finishing up around five and after I examine him again, we can get dinner or something," he added, as nonchalantly as possible.

Glancing nervously in the direction of Bernard, who was also outside watering plants the entire time, Donovan was sure he caught a smirk from the old man and hoped if he suspected anything was going on, he'd keep it to himself.

I have no idea what I'm doing.

CHAPTER 10

RILEY

After Donovan left, Riley, Bernard, and Scrappy went back in the house where Scrappy was glued to her side, awaiting her next move. Riley wasn't quite sure what the day would have in store, but coffee was a must.

"I trust you slept well?" Bernard asked.

"I did, thank you. I didn't realize quite how tired I was until I laid down for a moment with Scrappy. Next thing I knew, it was morning. It's a little strange sleeping somewhere that isn't my bed, but I fell right to sleep."

Bernard chuckled. "Well, my dear, it's been a rather overwhelming couple of days. Can I get you some breakfast?"

Riley pursed her lips. "I told you that you do not have to wait on me."

"I already made breakfast. I simply saved you some, is all," he replied with a suspicious smirk.

She knew that was probably only half true, but the grumble in her stomach said to let it go. "Well, if you already made it, then I would love some. But please, don't go to any trouble for me."

"I wouldn't dream of it," he replied.

"By the way, thank you so much for putting the food out last night while the vet and I were out on a walk. I wanted to see the water, I hadn't been down there yet. That was very nice of you, and so much more than we needed."

"It was my pleasure, Riley," he said. "That was very kind of the good doctor to come by, wasn't it?"

Riley had followed Bernard to the kitchen and sat at the large bar while he fixed up a plate of bacon, waffles, and berries for her. He handed her a cup of coffee before warming up the bacon. As she took a sip of the delicious brew, she couldn't help but grin sheepishly.

"It was rather nice, wasn't it?" she said. "Is that normal in this town? For the vet to come by and check on your pet? A house call didn't really seem necessary, but now I'm a little worried about the big goof." They had just been outside, letting Scrappy do his business and have a brief walk, when the doctor stopped by and said the pup might still have issues so he should get checked out again.

Bernard chuckled before saying, "I don't believe that it is, Riley. Dr. Hunter seems to have taken a special interest in… Scrappy." Finished making her breakfast, Bernard walked the plate over to the bar, setting it in front of her. He looked over at Scrappy, who was practically drooling, likely at the smell of bacon. "Okay, boy, you can have one piece. But you better not start begging."

Riley was certain the dog smiled as his tail began whipping furiously.

"Should we be giving him bacon?" she asked.

"Oh, I'm sure it's fine. We won't make a habit of giving him people food though. Sometimes I just can't resist that puppy face of his."

"He does kind of grow on you, doesn't he?"

"He sure does."

Bernard and Riley sat quietly while she ate, and the dog laid down at her feet on the cool tile floor.

"I thought I could give you and Scrappy a ride to see Dr. Hunter today," Bernard said, breaking the silence.

"That's not necessary," she replied.

"Oh, I know it's not. But I heard him mention getting dinner after your appointment, and wouldn't that be easier if I took Scrappy home?"

"Well, then how would I get home?" Riley asked, genuinely confused.

Bernard smirked. "I'm sure that the good doctor would bring you home. He only lives about two miles away from here."

Riley gave Bernard a sideways glance. "Now, why would he want to do that?" She set her coffee cup down and folded her arms across her chest.

"You *can* see the doctor is smitten with you, can't you?"

Her jaw dropped. "What are you talking about?" Truly confused, Riley immediately thought back to every interaction she'd had with Donovan thus far. "Do you think this is a *date*?" she asked, aghast.

A full-on belly laugh escaped Bernard, so boisterous Scrappy picked his head up off the floor lazily to see what was so funny. "Would that be so terrible?" he asked, still chuckling.

"Yes!" she exclaimed.

"Riley, you are too funny. What's the big deal? It's just dinner."

"Exactly. It's just dinner. It's not a date. You don't know what you're talking about. He's just being neighborly... right?" she asked, knowing she was wrong and realizing it at the same time.

"Neighborly is bringing over some cookies, or inviting someone to a dinner party to meet new friends," he replied, trying to contain the ongoing chuckle.

"This is not funny, Bernard." Riley was mortified. The veterinarian with the asshole friend, who asked her if she needed rides practically every time they met, wanted to go on a *date*? Searching through her memory bank, she couldn't recall the last time she went on a date, or even the last time she *wanted* to go on a date. She'd all but given up on men, after her last relationship ended in an embarrassing display of lechery she'd let slide, even though she knew the man she'd been dating for two years had been cheating on her every time he traveled for work.

"I don't mean to laugh, Riley, I'm sorry," he said. "But really, would it be so bad? Donovan is a very eligible bachelor, has a thriving practice here in Port Henry, and comes from a good family. I knew his mother quite well."

She buried her face in her hands before peeking through her fingers to look at Bernard. "But, a date? I don't even live here! It doesn't make any sense."

"You may not live here... yet. But this is your house. What you decide to do with it long-term is obviously something you have to figure out, but why not allow yourself to enjoy a bit of the time here and see if the Port suits you as much as I think it might. I know, with absolute certainty, that is what Jameson would have wanted."

"Oh, so you're going to play the 'deceased benefactor friend' card? Really?" she asked, placing her hands on her hips dramatically.

Bernard shrugged and grabbed the coffee pot to refill her mug. "I'm just saying, there's no reason why two attractive, young, and single people shouldn't have a meal together and enjoy each other's company. It doesn't have to be anything more than that."

"You know I'm not planning to stay here full-time."

"I know that you say this now, but I also know that you have an entire house to explore. You have time to check out Port Henry, and all it has to offer. Including single veterinarians who seem to like you... and your dog."

Riley's initial shock began to wore off, and as images of Donovan's smile conjured in her mind, a grin began to form and butterflies tickled her belly. He was ridiculously good-looking, and had shown a genuine interest in Scrappy. Maybe dinner with a handsome, clearly intelligent man wouldn't be the worst way to spend an evening. It didn't have to go anywhere after all. She thought maybe he'd be able to help her find Scrappy a new home when the time came too.

"Maybe you're right, Bernard," she conceded. "But, that doesn't mean that I'm staying, or that I'm keeping Scrappy. I still have a life in the city I'll need to get back to at some point."

"Of course," he replied as he cleaned up the breakfast dishes. The conversation was clearly over, they'd both made their points, and Riley had resigned that dinner with a hot dude that loved animals wasn't a terrible way to spend an evening. It could certainly be worse.

Riley wasn't sure what her big hurry to get back to the city was; in fact, she had no real reason to rush back. Jameson wanted her to stay for the summer, he said as much to his lawyer, but she couldn't help but feel like she wasn't in her own home, even if she did own it. She decided to spend the day back in Jameson's study, exploring. The photograph that she found and tucked back in the drawer was calling her name and she hoped she'd find an explanation for it as well.

Excusing herself, Riley headed to the study, Scrappy following her. *That dog wants to be with me all the damn time*, she thought. Riley shut the door behind them, not wanting to be interrupted, but also she didn't want Bernard to see her rifling through Jameson's desk, even if it was her prerogative.

Glancing around, everything seemed to be exactly how she'd left it the night before when Donovan showed up, so she sat back at the desk and pulled the drawer open that had contained the photos. As she rifled through them, she discovered the one she was looking for was missing.

It has to be here!

Her heart raced and she feverishly looked around the room, then checked the floor and rifled through the other drawers, thinking maybe she had shoved it somewhere else, even though she was quite sure it should've been right there.

Shit. Where could it be? She was panicking.

"Bernard," she whispered aloud. He had to have taken the picture. No one else was in the house, and she'd not left since she found it. But why would he take the photograph? He more than encouraged her to make everything in the house her own, as if he wanted her to find things. After tapping her fingers on the desk, mulling over the possibilities, she decided she'd wait to confront him. Surely, there were other clues in that house that would lead her to figure out what secrets Jameson had.

Closing the desk drawer, Riley got up and moved to the window where Scrappy had set himself up in the sunshine again. She sat down next to him and rubbed his exposed belly.

"What was he hiding, Scrappy?" she asked him.

The dog, of course, just glanced at her, panting and rolled around on his back to encourage more belly rubs. Riley let out a small laugh and continued to appease the beast. She'd never spent much time around dogs, having grown up in a pet-free home. But she couldn't help smiling at the dog's enthusiasm toward her.

She knew there had to be other things Jameson was hiding, and if they weren't in his office, they had to be somewhere else in the house. *But where?*

When she first arrived, Bernard had given her a basic tour of the house, and the room she was set up in was a very large guest suite adjacent to the master suite, which was Jameson's room. The door had been shut, and she'd not seen inside, but she realized that perhaps what she was looking for might be in that room. Riley continued rubbing Scrappy's belly and mulling over what she knew about Jameson.

She had never found out where he heard about her, and before this, that hadn't bothered her, but she was beginning to wonder if there was a far deeper connection she didn't understand. He hired her sight unseen, without much talk of references or prior work. There had to be a link somewhere. Since Bernard didn't seem to go to Jameson's old bedroom either, she decided to snoop there later, when she was sure he would be gone for a while and she wouldn't get caught. In the meantime, she decided the best next step in her mission to find the truth would be to go back through all of her book notes. The conversations she and Jameson had, the finished chapters, the pages and pages of notes that she took—something there had to be a clue.

Riley checked her watch, and seeing that she had plenty

of time to spend going back through her documentation before her date-not-a-date vet appointment, she took off to her room to grab her laptop, causing Scrappy to leap up and run toward the door as well.

"Okay, boy, let's go see what we can find out about your dad," she said quietly.

Scrappy gave her hand a small lick, leaving a trail of slobber behind.

Wiping her hand on her jeans, she muttered, "Gross," and opened the door so the two of them could head back upstairs.

CHAPTER 11

DONOVAN

"Scrappy is going to be in around five," Donovan said, not making eye contact with Toni.

"Why? Is there something new going on with him?"

"I just want to make sure all the things he ingested haven't caused any latent bowel obstructions or anything," he replied, continuing to evade the probing eyes he knew were skeptically staring at him.

"You sure you didn't want to just check in on the pretty new girl in town?" Toni said with a giggle.

"What? Why would you say that? I've been totally professional!" he exclaimed,

"I never said you weren't, Mr. Defensive. I'm merely suggesting that there's a pretty new rich girl in town, and she seems right up your alley."

"What would make you say that?" He couldn't help but

let a grin form as his friend and assistant called him out.

Toni tilted her head at him like a puppy would and placed one hand on her hip. "Seriously, Donovan? You don't think I know that it's almost summertime?"

"What does that mean?"

"Summer is when you and that shithead Gavin get your annual prowling on. It's when you let the patients flirt a little more, and you spend a little more time with the female owners than you need to."

Donovan was shocked, and his mouth fell open.

"Oh, pick your jaw up off the floor. You can't possibly be surprised that I know this. It's practically common knowledge that you're like a dormant hermit in the winter. All business. But when summer comes, you... let loose, shall we say?"

The implication that he was, in fact, one of the town gigolos had set in, and embarrassment swept through him. It wasn't who he'd ever intended to be, it was just the way things had panned out for him socially. His thoughts turned to Riley though, and he didn't want her to think that of him, causing mild panic. "I'm just making sure the dog is okay, Toni. I'm not prowling on Riley." He was sure he'd said it with enough confidence that it was almost believable.

"Listen, you don't owe me an explanation for what you do on your own time. I just think that you need to be careful with that girl. I don't think she has any idea what she's getting herself into," Toni replied.

"What's that supposed to mean?" Donovan was getting annoyed at the suggestion that something untoward was being plotted out by him. Especially when he found himself thinking of only her all damn day.

"Just that she's going through something. Anyone can see that. She was obviously close to Jameson Prescott for him to leave her literally everything he owned. She seems exasperated and I've only just met her once. Overnight, she became one of the wealthiest people in the Port, and you can see in her eyes she doesn't have any idea what that means." Toni paused and scrutinized Donovan's concerned face. "I'm just saying, Donovan, that she probably needs a friend. Not an eligible *bachelor* that wants to get in her pants."

Crinkling his eyebrows at her, he audibly huffed. "I'll have you know that I had no intention of trying to get in her pants," he lied. Men were always going to be interested in sex, whether they meant to be or not, and in Donovan's case, he wasn't specifically trying to get Riley into bed. He just wanted to keep her in the Port for the summer if he could.

"Is that why you scheduled her *on your own* to come at the end of the day, on the one day a week you know I leave at four thirty to meet my trainer? You knew I wouldn't be here." She continued to give him a skeptical glare.

"That was just a fortunate coincidence," he replied, unable to contain the chuckle.

Toni chuckled back, shaking her head. "Is there even anything wrong with that damn dog?"

"There could be?" he replied, with a questioning tone and a shrug.

Toni rolled her eyes, and handed him a folder. "Mrs. Covington is here with the hot dogs."

"They're daschunds." He grinned.

"They're hot dogs, and they need their vaccines. So, chop-chop, loverboy."

Donovan took the folder and headed into the exam room, chuckling to himself. He adored Toni and her candor, even if his bullshit was getting called out. "Good morning, Mrs. Covington, how are Trixie and Crystal?" he asked as he shut the door behind him.

. . .

THE REST of the day was uneventful and Donovan tried not to let the anxiety in his chest give him a heart attack as five o'clock approached. He tugged at the neck of his undershirt, feeling warm as the clock ticked. Toni had left for the day, giving him what he called the fish eye on her way out, to which he couldn't help but laugh a little. She knew him better than he thought, and in that moment, he wasn't sure he loved being so transparent, and hoped his nerves weren't as obvious to Riley.

He hadn't considered that it was sort of a date until he let his mind wander into overdrive, but thought better of it when he remembered she would have Scrappy with her. All the other patients had left for the day when he heard the chime of the bell on the glass door, and the distinctive bark of the Great Dane shortly after. Chuckling, he got up from his desk and walked out to the lobby, where he found Riley bearing down, holding his leash with all her strength so he wouldn't run from her.

"Hi there," he said, trying not to sound too excited.

Just as she was about to reply, her mouth open, the excitement of seeing Donovan gave Scrappy just enough extra strength to pull Riley forward, launching her directly into his chest as the leash wound around the two of them, pulling them together. Without thought, his arms wrapped around her as the dog circled them, tying them up in place. Instantly, Donovan smelled her perfume—or maybe it was her shampoo—a combination of coconut and jasmine, and as he inhaled, the scent left him intoxicated, making him forget that a giant dog had bound them together unintentionally. Until Riley started to wriggle, trying to get loose, did Donovan realize they were stuck.

"Shit!" she exclaimed.

"Hold still, I'll grab his leash and unhook it," Donovan

said, laughing as he reached for Scrappy's collar. Grabbing Scrappy's collar turned out to be more difficult than he'd expected, as the dog seemed to be enjoying the game, and dragged the two, still locked tightly together, toward the front counter as he bounced around them.

"Oh my God, you've gotta be kidding me," she muttered, holding onto Donovan, trying to remain upright.

"Don't worry, I'll get it," he replied. Having her pressed against him was making his heart race and the combination of her exhilarating scent made it hard to concentrate on separating them while the dog continued to excitedly jump up and down. If he didn't know any better, he'd have thought Scrappy did it on purpose, in which case he'd have to remember to give him some treats. *Back to the issue at hand,* he thought. "Scrappy, *sit!*" he bellowed, causing Riley to jump and bury her face in his chest.

Stay focused.

Scrappy had formal training, even if you wouldn't know it most of the time, and did obey commands. He immediately sat, likely awaiting a treat for good behavior.

"Good boy." Donovan's tone was softer now as he reached over and unhooked the leash from the dog's collar. "I'm sorry, I didn't mean to scare you," he said to Riley as he began to loosen the leash from around them.

"Oh God, I'm fine. I didn't realize he would listen to commands. I'm so sorry he did that." She covered her face with her now free hand. Seeming embarrassed, she quickly helped Donovan unbind them from each other and stepped back.

Donovan laughed. "It's fine. He takes some getting used to." Looking over at Scrappy, who was still sitting patiently as instructed, he shook his head. "His breed can be clumsy and hard to keep control of, but he's a good boy."

"Yeah, a good boy." She glared at the dog.

An uncomfortable silence passed over them and Donovan cleared his throat. "Um, let's go on back and take a look at this guy. Come on, Scrappy," he said, waving the leash ahead of him so Scrappy would go.

"So, do you think he's gonna be okay?" Riley asked quietly, seeming exasperated.

Donovan thought for a moment, debating what to say. On one hand, the dog seemed perfectly fine, and it wasn't the first time he'd eaten a bunch of garbage. But, on the other hand, he was running out of excuses to see Riley, and the dog was his in with her. *You can't keep examining this dog like something's wrong with him. Get her out to dinner and make a move.* Giving himself a pep talk silently, he decided using the dog was only going to last for so long, and the bad karma of bringing Scrappy in when he wasn't sick probably wasn't a good idea anyway.

He smiled. "I think he's going to be just fine." She sighed, presumably in relief, and rested her hands on the exam table. "Are you going to be okay?" he asked, placing a hand on top of hers.

Riley looked down at their hands before meeting his glance. With tear-filled eyes, she whispered, "I don't know."

A stabbing pain in his chest overtook him at the sight of her obvious pain and without a further thought, he grabbed her wrist and pulled her to him, embracing her in a hug. Arms wrapped completely around her, he held her tightly, wanting to absorb the pain she was feeling. At first, she stood motionless, then relaxed into him, letting the sobs come out as she buried her face in his chest for the second time that afternoon.

Donovan didn't know how much time had passed, but he consoled her, stroking her hair, holding her, until her sobs turned to smaller sniffles, then stopped all together. She'd held onto him as she cried, and when her hands loosened around his back, he wanted to pull her closer, but let her break their embrace.

"Jesus Christ," she said, rubbing her face with her hands. "I'm a fucking mess. I'm so sorry, Dr. Hunter." She rolled her eyes and nervously laughed as she increased the distance between them.

Donovan took a step closer. "First of all, it's Donovan. Not Dr. Hunter." He reached out for her hand, which she gave to him as she watched him closely. As he placed her hand over his heart, he said, "And you're not a mess. You lost someone that you cared about, you inherited an entirely new life, and a dog. A crazy, giant dog. I'd say you're entitled to a meltdown." He laughed, hoping it would lighten the mood while also expressing his understanding of all she'd been going through.

"Thank you," she replied, smiling.

"What do you say we go get some food, and I'll show you around the neighborhood?" he asked.

Taking her hand back and glancing over at Scrappy, who was patiently watching them, she said, "I don't know. I have to get him home—"

Donovan cut her off. "You and I both know Bernard is outside waiting to take Scrappy home for you." His advance knowledge of Bernard's offer had come in handy. "So, let's deliver him to Bernard and I'll get you home later." He grinned, pleased with himself and knowing she had no other excuses not to come with him.

A defeated smile spread across her lips. "Okay, you win."

CHAPTER 12

RILEY

Feeling like a fool for her breakdown, Riley let Donovan take Scrappy out to the car, so he could go home while she went to the restroom to clean herself up. Mostly, she just wanted to blow her nose; all the crying had her feeling like her nose would never stop running, and she needed to see just how bad she looked.

After freshening up, she stared at herself in the mirror of the one-person bathroom. A poster advertising the spay and neuter program in the background drew her attention, and the cartoon tomcat that looked like he was going on a date made her laugh. *What is wrong with you? You don't even know this guy, and you just snotted all over his shirt.* She shook her head, grabbed some lip gloss out of her purse, and touched up her lips. If she was going to go out to dinner with him after that hot mess, she might as well fix up what was left of her makeup.

When she walked out of the bathroom, Donovan was waiting for her, leaning against the wall across from the door. He grinned and said, "You ready?"

Hesitantly, she replied, "I think so."

He walked ahead of her, opening the door, then stopping behind her to lock up the front entrance. Her eyes had drifted down his broad shoulders to his round ass, filling out his jeans. As her heart rate picked up, she grinned at her attraction to him. It had been so long since she'd paid any attention to a man, and the fact that Donovan was taking her out after her crying jag was almost unbelievable to her. He had to have his pick of all the women in that town, so why her? She chalked it up to being the new girl in town; after all, Port Henry wasn't that big and the summer season rush of people hadn't quite started yet. It was quiet in the little town, but Bernard had told her traffic would increase in a matter of about two weeks, and the shops and restaurants would be overrun with tourists.

But on this night, it was quiet in a peaceful way.

Donovan opened the door to his Escalade for her, making sure she could get in using the little step to the lifted SUV. "Thank you," she replied, before he closed the door and made his way around to the driver's side.

Once settled, he put the car in reverse and glanced over at her. "Is there anything in particular you *don't* like to eat?"

In her usual, self-deprecating way, she replied, "You don't get an ass like this being picky about food." She let out a nervous laugh, but Donovan didn't join in.

In fact, he turned serious and gently grabbed her wrist to gain her attention. Sheepishly, she met his gaze. "Riley Maxwell, you have a fine ass. And don't ever let anyone tell you otherwise." His tone was serious, almost gruff, sending chills down her spine as she took in just how manly he was. *Sexy. That's what it was.*

Unable to reply, her voice disappeared in awe of him, she simply nodded.

"Okay then," he said, grinning. "If you are not particular, then I'll take you to one of my favorite places. Trust me, you'll love it."

"I trust you," she said quietly.

THEY RODE in silence but for the radio playing Top Forty quietly. She listened as Donovan hummed along to the hits of the week, smiling at how relaxed and happy he seemed. When they pulled in, a large neon sign read *Hank's Fish Tank*. The exterior looked like a giant fishing boat, complete with old-fashioned life preservers, and a rope walkway to the entrance.

When he helped her out of the car, he didn't let go of her hand as they walked toward the restaurant. "Now, I know it doesn't look like much, it's kind of kitschy, but I swear to you, they have the best seafood in town, and they'll take good care of us."

Riley's stomach growled as the aroma of freshly cooked seafood wafted over them. She glanced down at their joined hands, confused, but not hating it. "Sounds good," she replied.

Donovan led her inside, walking past the hostess station, which was unmanned anyway. They continued walking through the restaurant, which was about half full, until they reached the very back, where another set of doors led outside to a patio, filled with more tables. As Riley looked around at the rustic decor, Donovan directed her to a table overlooking the water against the very back of the patio. After pulling her chair out, he waved to a server, who came over almost immediately.

"Donovan! It's been forever, how are you?" An older woman, around her mid-sixties, came over and hugged him energetically. Riley wasn't sure what to do, but the woman's enthusiasm was contagious, and she smiled at their interaction.

"Margie, I'm great. I've just been super busy. But, I've brought a fr– Uh, this is Riley. She's new to Port Henry," he introduced her.

Riley tried to stand, but Margie gently held her shoulder to keep her sitting. "Don't get up, dear. It's lovely to meet you. How are you liking Port Henry so far?" she asked.

Clearing her throat, Riley replied, "I... uh... so far, it's really nice. I've only been here a couple of days."

"Well, the fun is just beginning, you know. The summer crowd will be here soon, and us townies will have to find a way to survive the crowds. You'll be here all summer then, right?"

Donovan didn't let her answer. "I'm actually working on that now." He winked at Margie, then smiled down at Riley. "She's yet to see all that the Port has to offer, so I had to bring her to my favorite spot for dinner before selling her on spending the summer with us."

Margie laughed emphatically. "Well, if anyone has learned to love the Port over time, it's this guy right here." She patted Donovan on the shoulder. "Now sit, young man. I'll grab you guys some water and our famous biscuits, and have one of the girls come over and take care of you."

"Thanks, Margie," Donovan said.

"Thank you," Riley offered as well.

Donovan took his seat and grinned. "So, that's Margie.

She was married to Hank, of"—he raised his hands, gesturing at the room—"the Fish Tank."

"Was?" Riley asked.

"Oh, yeah. He passed away a few years ago and she kept running the place. Her kids grew up here, and went to school with me. Her son and I graduated from high school together, he's the manager now. His sister Janine became a chef and came back to run the kitchen. They've got a great thing going here."

Donovan's enthusiasm was contagious, and she found herself smiling as he told her the story of the restaurant and the people who worked there. He made a few recommendations on the menu, although everything looked amazing, and Riley couldn't wait to try it all. Ordering far more food than they could possibly have eaten, Donovan handed the menus back to the server and stood up, holding his hand out to her.

"Come on," he said.

"Where are we going?" she asked, grinning.

"Just give me your hand." He dramatically stuck his out again for her to take.

Laughing, she took it and he immediately pulled her toward the side of the room, through a door she hadn't noticed before. Leading her outside, the rush of cool air coming off the water hit her, giving her a chill.

Pulling her close, he wrapped an arm around her as he leaned against a balcony overlooking the water. Through the windows behind them was the dining room, but outside was a massive view of the bay. The setting sun cast an orange glow across the sky, illuminating the gentle waves over the water.

"Sorry, I didn't realize it would still be chilly out here," he said.

Nestling into him a bit, soaking up his warmth, she replied, "It's not that bad."

He squeezed her gently as they watched the sun fade completely and only a faint light shone over the water. "Come on, let's get back inside."

They made their way back to the table, just in time for Hank's "famous" cheddar biscuits. Riley assumed they would taste like the kind she'd had a seafood chain once that were good, but nothing special, and she was more than happy to be proven wrong. Warm from the oven, the buttermilk biscuits had gooey cheddar, Old Bay seasoning, and some other ingredients she couldn't place, but loved every bite. Remembering that they had more food coming, she had to restrain herself from eating more than one. Okay, maybe two.

"They're amazing, right?" Donovan smiled and nodded knowingly.

"They really are," she said, laughing. "This was a good pick."

"Thank you. I'm glad you like it." He leaned back in his chair, watching her.

"What?" Riley asked, grabbing a napkin and dabbing it at her face. "Do I have something on my face?"

Donovan leaned forward and took the napkin from her. Chuckling, he said, "No, you don't have anything on your face. I was just looking at you." He set the napkin down on the table. "You're beautiful."

Unused to compliments that bold, Riley's eyes bulged. She didn't know what to say and felt self-conscious, suddenly remembering what Bernard had said. *I'm on a date. Fuck. What am I supposed to say?*

"Thank you?" She didn't mean for it to sound like a question, but it did. Her discomfort must have been evident, because Donovan quickly spoke up again.

"You're welcome, but that's not why I said it. I was just making an observation," he replied casually. Changing the subject, he asked, "Are you feeling better?"

Grateful for the topic change, even though it still meant she had to express herself as tongue-tied as she was, she replied, "Listen, I am so sorry for breaking down in your office. I'm a little bit lost right now, to be completely honest. I don't know what I'm supposed to do here. It feels like I'm on a sad vacation, squatting in someone else's house."

Donovan didn't reply right away, just leaned forward and took her hand again. He'd been doing that a lot, she thought. Running his thumb over the inside of her hand, he smiled. "It's your house. And if you're lost, I can show you around. If you'll accept a ride from me, that is."

A giggle escaped and Riley smiled gratefully at him. "Thank you."

"You know what else?" he asked.

"What?" she replied, on the edge of her seat.

"What you're *supposed* to do... is whatever the fuck you want to do."

As if it were planned, the massive amount of food that they ordered arrived, causing them to separate their hands to make room for all the plates. Riley sat speechless, taking in what he said.

The question is, what the fuck do I want to do?

CHAPTER 13

DONOVAN

He knew taking her to Hank's was the way to go. It wasn't crowded and they could talk as much or as little as they wanted. Not to mention the fact that the food was amazing. Every time he grabbed her hand in his, it felt perfect, like it was made to be there. But, after Riley's upset in his office, he thought long and hard about what Toni had said. *That girl needs a friend.*

But Donovan didn't want to be her friend. Briefly, he considered who he knew in town so he could find her one, anyone but him. *Maybe she and Toni could be friends.* He reconsidered that idea after some more thought. Regardless of what Toni said swirling in the back of his mind, when Riley was near, he craved her closeness, and wanted more. Like an addict who couldn't get enough, once he touched her, he kept trying to find more ways to be in physical contact with her.

He'd reached out to take her hand numerous times at the restaurant, and not once did she pull away. While his mind buzzed with the what should I do's where it came to her, they continued to share pleasant dinner conversation and kept things light. Once they'd finished, and were sufficiently stuffed to the gills, Donovan asked if she wanted to go home, or if she'd like to go out to the beach.

"It might be a little cold on the beach," she said wistfully.

"Well, I need to let my dogs out, so how about if we stop by my place, and I'll give you a hoodie," he offered. Genuinely not wanting her to think it was a slimy way to get her back to his place, he added, "I have two dogs and they've been inside all day. No shenanigans, I promise." He raised his hands in innocence, making her laugh.

"Let's get out of here," he said, pulling out his wallet to pay.

"Let me," she offered.

Brought up a gentleman when it came to these sorts of things, Donovan would never let her pay. He didn't care how many houses she inherited, or if the mattresses were stuffed with hundred dollar bills. He asked her out, and he'd be paying.

"That's never going to happen," he replied, smirking.

"Are you sure? I apparently have a lot of money," she said, laughing.

"That's the word on the street, and yes, I'm sure. My mother would kill me if I even considered it, which I did not," he added. "Now, let's go. My dogs are probably dancing around with their legs crossed."

Riley laughed again, a sound he wanted to hear more of, like a rock ballad you jam to on the radio. Her laugh was melodic, and making her laugh lifted his spirits in return.

A short drive later, they pulled into Donovan's driveway. As they got out of the SUV, they could hear both hounds barking away, recognizing their dad's vehicle. Riley stood hesitantly on the porch while Donovan opened the door and greeted the pups.

Assuming she was right behind him, he looked for her then ran back outside. "Well, come on, it's chilly out there. Get in here," he insisted.

Riley followed him in, casually glancing around. Similarly to Jameson's mansion, Donovan's house had giant glass panes along the back of the home, leading out to the beach and what looked like a big deck in the back as well. He quickly ran to the back door and opened it, letting the dogs run outside, and then came back in to check on her.

"You okay?" he asked.

"I am," she said, smiling softly.

Grabbing her hand and squeezing it briefly, he said, "I'll grab us both a hoodie, and then we can head outside. You want to grab us a drink of some kind?"

"Sure, that would be great. What would you like?"

"I'll have bourbon. There's plastic cups in the cupboard next to the sink, and anything you might be in the mood for as well. I'll be back in a sec," he said, rushing up the stairs to the second floor.

He raced to his room, not wanting to leave her alone for too long, for fear she'd change her mind and want to go home. There was no way he wanted that to happen. While he hadn't settled upon whether or not he could handle *being friends*, he wanted to spend more time with her either way, and the beach made everyone relax. The bourbon didn't hurt.

Donovan grabbed his favorite New York University hoodie and sniffed it, making sure it was clean, but also checking to see if it smelled like him. Giving her his favorite hoodie, knowing full well he might never get it back, brought a childlike grin to his face. *Why do I feel like I'm in high school all over again? Ugh, I'm so nervous.* Confident that it sufficiently smelled like his cologne, he grabbed a different one for himself and threw it over his head before brushing his teeth super fast and back running downstairs.

Riley was in the kitchen, with both dogs at her feet. "I don't know where your food is guys, I'm sorry," she was saying to them. The whimpers that followed caused Donovan to laugh, announcing his presence.

"They trying to get you to pour them a drink too?" he asked, chuckling.

"I think they're hungry?" she replied questioningly.

"They probably are," he said, walking toward the pantry door. He handed Riley the sweatshirt before getting the dogs' food out. "This is for you, that should keep you warm."

Just like he thought she would, she brought it up to her face, inhaling casually as if he didn't know what she was doing. As a grin spread, she pulled it over her head and down her body, distracting him from the hungry dogs. Way too big for her, she looked like she was wearing a cozy blanket as she hugged herself in the warm sweatshirt.

"Aren't you supposed to be feeding these poor dogs? What kind of vet are you?" she teased him.

Completely stunned, Donovan stood motionless, reeling from her joke. When she started laughing, he came to his senses and filled the dogs' bowls, laughing himself. "Did you find everything okay?" he asked.

"I did, thank you." She walked toward him and handed him a plastic cup with way more bourbon than anyone needed as a nightcap. "You don't mix anything with bourbon, right?"

"Well, maybe if you're going to drink a trough of it like this, you might, but not usually," he joked.

"I don't know anything about bourbon," she said, laughing.

"Well, if I didn't know any better, I'd think you were trying to get me drunk," he replied.

When she just shrugged her shoulders and took a sip of her equally full cup, his heart started to race again.

Fuck, what am I doing? I'm definitely flirting with her, and she's flirting back. I'm supposed to be a nice guy. Nice guys don't do that, do they? Sure they do, nice guys flirt with beautiful women all the time. He convinced himself that flirting was harmless, and since she wasn't running for the door, it was all good.

"Do you want to go check out the water, then maybe come back up to the deck and sit in front of the firepit?" he offered.

"Sounds great," she replied.

Donovan gestured for her to go ahead of him out the back door, leaving the dogs in the kitchen scarfing down their food. He unlocked the doggie door before they left, so the pooches could see themselves out if they wanted, and he wouldn't have to worry about it. The wind had picked up a bit, and while it was almost summer, the cool spring air continued to have a chill in the evening.

"Are you warm enough?" he asked her when they stopped to take their shoes off at the end of the wooden path, just before stepping out into the sand.

"I am. Thank you for the sweatshirt, it's pretty cozy." She winked. "You might not get it back."

"Well, it's my favorite, so if you take it, that just means that we have to go out again," he countered.

"Seems fair," she replied, stepping out onto the cool sand.

Following behind her, Donovan chuckled. Totally at a

loss for what to do, he decided to go with the flow. *Fuck it. What's the worst that can happen?*

The water in and around the Atlantic Ocean was far too cold to put your feet in just yet, but the hardened sand that had been soaked earlier when the tide was in was solid enough that they didn't sink with every step. They walked along the shoreline quietly for a bit before she stopped to face him, setting her cup in the sand at her feet.

"Is everything all right?" he asked.

"I think so," she replied.

"You're not sure?"

"I'll know in a minute," she replied quietly, moving closer to him, slowly dragging her hands toward his hips before they settled near his ribs. Even through the sweatshirt, her touch sent shivers through him, and he wasn't sure what to do next.

Donovan's hands rested at his sides, one holding his cup of bourbon, the other forming a fist as he tried to fight the urge to pounce on her. "What are you doing?" he whispered, barely audible. In his head, he knew where this was going, but his desire to tread lightly was causing a hurricane to brew inside.

The reflection of the waves was just barely visible in her eyes as the bright moon shone over them. As she stared into his, he was certain she could hear his heart about to beat right through his chest.

"Do you want to kiss me?" she asked.

Are you fucking kidding me? Fuck yes, I want to kiss you. Wait! Wait one second. What would a nice guy say? Sonofabitch. I have no idea what a nice guy would say.

A "what do I do now" nervous chuckle escaped as his hands casually found their way to her shoulders, still holding his cup of bourbon. "Do you want me to kiss you?" he asked tentatively, hoping he was right in assuming where this line of questioning was going. Riley's hands squeezed him just a bit harder, and he stepped as close as he could while still leaving her room to answer. Their bodies were pressed together as she looked up at him towering over her short frame. Donovan felt himself grinning, giving exactly zero fucks about how ridiculous the shit-eating grin he wore looked.

"Yes, please." She barely got the words out when Donovan tossed his cup aside, taking her face in his hands and crushing his lips to hers. The kiss was everything he'd imagined it would be, and he practically consumed her as she wrapped her arms around his waist completely, holding him tight to her. When a small moan escaped her lips, he scooped her up, then set her gently in the sand, covering her with his body.

He pulled away just long enough to look at her and catch her smile before he leaned down again, pressing his lips to hers. Their tongues swirled together, and as the kisses deepened, she ran her hand along his chest, up toward his neck and into the back of his hair. Her touch was electric. Before things went too far, not that they could with all the clothes they had on, and the cool air, Donovan pulled away, propping himself up over her.

"Is something wrong?" she asked, bringing a hand to her full lips.

"Are you kidding me?" he replied. "Of course not." He leaned down to give her a soft, tender kiss.

She let out a nervous laugh. "Then why aren't you kissing me?"

Donovan rolled over onto his back, staring up at the sky. He sighed deeply and turned toward her. "If you keep kissing me like that out here, I'm not going to be able to stop and we can't have the neighbors watching us, now can we?" He grinned and reached over, pulling her face to his, planting another soft, sensual kiss on her lips.

Riley giggled before getting quiet again. Lying on their sides in the cool sand of late spring, she ran her thumb over Donovan's bottom lip. "How about one more kiss before we go back?"

Happy to oblige, he thought.

CHAPTER 14

RILEY

Riley couldn't even remember the last time she kissed a man with such passion and fervor, but she was certain if she had, it never felt like kissing Donovan. He was every bit a man, taking her in his arms, devouring her like he was starved for her touch. It was all she could do to keep from having him take her right there on the beach, even though she knew that would be a mistake.

When she agreed to go home with Donovan, she wasn't sure what she wanted to do. Her plans hadn't changed, but it occurred to her on the drive over that she had no plan. The plan was whatever she wanted it to be. After their hot and heavy make out session in the sand, they playfully walked hand in hand back to his house. When they stepped on the porch, the heated moment had passed, and Riley wasn't especially certain what came next. She wanted to sleep with him, that wasn't even a question, but with everything going on in her life, she couldn't help but wonder if she should.

It turned out not to be an issue, as Donovan took the lead on what would happen next. They approached the house and once they had grabbed their shoes and made it to the deck, he stopped abruptly, turning her toward him.

"I can't believe I'm saying this, but I think I should take you home," he said.

Both relief and disappointment washed over her. "Are you sure? I can stay," she offered.

Donovan let go of her and paced the back deck, walking back and forth running a hand through his hair. "No, I'm not sure at all," he replied, a chuckle escaping.

"Are you okay?" she asked, confused by his behavior. She was pretty sure he wanted her a few minutes ago, if the bulge pressing against her was any indication.

He stopped and in two large strides was back in front of her. Cupping her face in his hands, he leaned down to kiss her, stoking the building fire between them again. Riley ran her hands just barely under the hem of the sweatshirt he wore, gently tracing her nails along his torso. As he sucked in a breath, he pulled away, panting, still clutching her face.

He rested his forehead against hers and wrapped his arms around her. She could feel the beat of his heart as laid her palms against his chest and closed her eyes. His arms kept her warm, but more than that, they comforted her. Riley hadn't realized just how alone she'd been feeling, until she suddenly wasn't. While they stood on the back deck in silence, listening to the waves crashing in the distance, Riley could feel Donovan's heart rate slow down as they relaxed, just holding each other quietly.

Finally, he lifted his head and looked down at her. "You know that I want you, right?"

Riley had a choice. She could be a typical, needy girl and tell him she had no way of knowing that, he should prove it, or she could be mature, with a grown man, and tell him the truth.

"Yes," she said, opting for the truth, a small smile forming at the corners of her mouth.

Donovan sighed. "Thank fuck," he said.

"What is going on with you?" she asked, confused by his odd behavior.

He stepped back a bit, making sure she was looking him in the eyes. "Riley, I am so into you. I don't know what it is, I can't explain it. I don't even care what it is. But there's something special about you, and I am not gonna be that guy."

"What guy? What are you talking about?" He was rambling nonsense.

"The guy that goes out with you one fucking time and takes you to bed. I don't want to be that guy to you." He seemed exasperated, like it was difficult for him to say.

Sensing that he needed to hear her say something, Riley offered, "Donovan, it was just a kiss. It doesn't have to be anything more than that. Relax. You seem super wound up about this." She stepped back, breaking the physical connection they had.

Donovan grabbed her wrist, stopping her from moving any further away. "It wasn't just a kiss and you know it." His tone shifted from desperation, to hurt.

Appeasing him slightly, she replied, "Maybe it wasn't *just* a kiss." She refused to make eye contact, feeling a laugh coming on, and she tried to look away so he couldn't see it.

"I see you smiling," he said playfully.

"You're being really weird," she spun around and replied.

"I am. I agree. I'm not myself but that's a good thing. I

promise," he said. "Let me take you home. But promise me that you'll go out with me again?"

"You want to go out with me again?" she asked sarcastically.

"You know that I do. That's why you're wearing my sweatshirt home." He grinned. "Otherwise, I'll have to make up reasons for you to bring your dog in to see me," he added.

Tilting her head quizzically, she squinted her eyes at him. "Did my dog even need to see you today?"

A huge grin formed across his face. "Well, you see…"

"Oh my God! Don't you take an oath or something! You can't be lying about my dog so I'll come see you! What the fuck, Donovan!" she exclaimed, swatting at him.

"Listen, if you'd seen how hot you were the first day we met, you'd have done it too. That's all I'm saying." He raised his hands in surrender. "In my defense, I couldn't keep doing it, because I knew it was bad karma. Plus, your dog is like a bull in a China shop," he said.

"I cannot believe you lied so I'd bring that goddamn dog in. Do you know how hard he is for me to manage? We practically weigh the same. I could saddle him and ride him to your office." She stopped ranting, and began laughing. Donovan started laughing as well, and the two carried on about it until Donovan promised not to lie to her ever again.

"Bernard is the one that told me he could take Scrappy home so we could go out to dinner, he's the one you should be mad at," Donovan tried to deflect the blame.

"Listen, I have enough problems with Bernard, I don't need him meddling in whatever this is," she said, motioning between them.

"What's going on with Bernard?" Donovan asked, concern in his voice.

"Nothing in particular, except that he knows more about

Jameson, and what he was hiding, than he's letting on, and I don't like it." The tone of the evening had shifted yet again, and this time, not in a good way. Riley was ready for Donovan to take her home, and made it known as she walked past him to the kitchen where she'd left her purse. "I'm ready to go home now."

"I'm sorry, Riley, I didn't mean to pry."

Realizing it wasn't Donovan's fault that Bernard had secrets, she softened. "No, it's okay. I'm sorry I snapped at you. This is turning out to be kind of a weird day. Let's go?" she asked.

"Of course," he replied, grabbing his keys off the counter.

The short ride back to Jameson's old house, Riley's house, was quiet. Riley could feel the tension that had built between them, but she didn't know how to fix it, and wasn't sure if it was even worth it. After all, she hadn't yet decided how long she'd be in Port Henry. If they weren't going to sleep together and have a fling, or a one-night stand, or whatever it was that didn't happen, was there any point in continuing the flirtation? She mulled it over as the houses along the road got larger until they reached hers.

Donovan pulled into the driveway and turned off the headlights. Stopped in front of the house, neither spoke until he finally broke the silence. "Riley, look at me?" he asked.

Begrudgingly, she shifted her body to face him.

"Tonight was awesome. Please let me take you out again? I know it got kind of weird, and I promise it won't be like that again. You're just so… unexpected," he said.

What a strange thing to say. Unexpected. What does that even mean?

"How about this? I'm gonna keep this favorite sweatshirt of yours. So, I guess we'll have to go out again." She smirked at him.

"Deal," he replied. "Now, please scoot over here and kiss me again before I watch you walk away?"

The butterflies returned. Just like that.

Riley undid her seatbelt and moved as close as she could, leaning over the console. Donovan's large hand rose up, caressing her neck as he pulled her to him, gently sucking her bottom lip. The overwhelming urge to crawl on his lap so she could feel his hardness pressing against her was only tamed as she roughly gripped the front of his shirt in her hand, and just barely so once he ran his hand into the hair at the back of her neck, softly tugging at it as his tongue danced with hers.

They continued their goodnight kiss until this time, Riley was the one to pull away. Panting, she said, "I think I should go inside."

Pulling her back to him, Donovan nodded. "You should," he replied, coming in for another kiss, almost breathless. She reciprocated, but only for a moment.

"I don't want to stop kissing you," she said, resting her forehead against his. She'd been trying to make herself exit the vehicle, but her body wasn't cooperating. It couldn't get enough of him.

"I've never felt a kiss like this before," he admitted quietly.

"I thought it was just me," she whispered.

"Definitely not just you."

Riley felt herself grin with excitement.

"Tomorrow, let's spend the day together," he asked.

"Don't you have to work?"

"I'll tell my boss I need the day off," he said, letting out a little chuckle.

"I'd like that," she replied.

Donovan sat back, taking Riley's hands into his. "I'll call Toni in the morning and reschedule what I have. There was nothing serious on the calendar, so it shouldn't be a problem. I'll take you around town and give you a proper tour. Does that sound good?"

She squeezed his hands and replied excitedly, "I'd love that."

"Okay, then it's a date." Donovan's smile broadened, and he brought Riley's hands to his lips, kissing them softly. "On one condition," he added.

"What's that?" she asked.

"More of this amazing kissing. Lots more," he said, yanking her toward him, over the console and onto his lap in the driver's seat. "Do we have a deal, Miss Maxwell?" he asked, wrapping his arms around her waist as she straddled him seductively.

"We have a deal, Dr. Hunter," she said, right before leaning in for one more kiss.

They'd fogged the windows of the Escalade up so much that Donovan had to turn his defroster on full blast so he could see out the window to drive home. Riley let herself out of the SUV, climbing the rest of the way over him and out the driver's side door. Grinning the entire way up the walk, she slid her key in the lock and turned around one last time before going inside. Donovan was watching her intently it seemed, and gave her a small wave before she let herself in and shut the door behind her.

Standing in the foyer, her back against the front door, she listened as he pulled away, waiting until the sound of his car was no longer audible from where she stood. In his absence, reality set in as she glanced around the silent, large house before trekking up the stairs to her bedroom.

CHAPTER 15

DONOVAN

Toni was more than happy to take the day off, calling all of the patients and getting them scheduled for other days. When she asked him why he was taking a day off all of a sudden, he considered feigning illness, then thought better of it. She knew him too well, and she'd pry, so the new and improved Donovan told her the truth. After defending himself over the "she needs a friend" debate and a stern lecture, Toni wished him well and took care of the rescheduling while Donovan figured out what the day would hold.

They hadn't set any specific plans, but he knew it had to be good if he was going to convince her to stay in Port Henry. Originally, the plan had just been for the summer, but once they kissed, he was consumed with the idea of keeping her around. *What do nice guys do to win the girl*, he asked himself as he paced through the kitchen. Then, it hit him.

While it had been a cold evening out on the beach, the days were getting warm and the forecast called for nothing but sunny skies that day. At the end of the island was a beach that you could drive your vehicle on. Donovan hadn't been there in years, not since he and his mother went when he was small, but it held a special place for him and it was fun to do. He settled on a good old-fashioned beach day after some shopping in the square near the spot he was thinking of. Canterbury Beach didn't have any houses, it was strictly for fishing and surfing, and while he didn't do either of those things, it was peaceful. And romantic.

Donovan picked up his phone to text Riley.

Morning, Gorgeous, he started to type out. *Does that sound too lame? She is gorgeous though. Ugh, why is this so hard? Maybe I should just say good morning and leave it at that. But I want to compliment her.*

Donovan spent a full ten minutes running his hand through his thick, dark hair, trying to figure out how to say good morning to Riley. Finally, he settled on, *Good morning, you ready for a day of fun in the sun?* He rolled his eyes at himself and glanced down to the pair of dogs staring at him.

"What?" he asked them. "You saw her. She's fucking perfect. We need her to like us. You want her to stay, don't you?" Archie and Veronica, who were standing, watching him pace and talk to himself, sat down at attention upon hearing the command, "Stay." Donovan laughed, and got them each a biscuit for obeying the accidental command, when his phone dinged with an incoming message.

RILEY: I'm ready when you are. What should I wear? What are we doing?

. . .

HE GRINNED, unable to quell the excitement of getting to spend the whole day with her.

Donovan: We're going to go down to the edge of the island, do some shopping, hang out on the beach, eat. Sound good?

Riley: Looking forward to it.

Donovan: Me too. I'll be over in a half hour to pick you up, will that work?

Riley: See you then

DONOVAN STARED at the phone in his hand, debating if he should say anything else. Opting to wait, he slid the phone in his pocket and headed to the pantry. While he was a bachelor, he did live in an affluent town, with unique local businesses. Not the least of which were local honey, cheese, and wine shops. He grabbed what he had, setting it all on the counter before turning to the dogs.

"Don't touch it. I'm going to get a cooler out of the garage. I'm gonna be super pissed if you take my picnic," he warned them. Veronica and Archie, much like the characters they were named after, glanced at each other before looking back at him. He was certain that if dogs could shrug, the two of them would have.

He quickly rummaged through some things in the garage, looking for the small cooler on wheels that he kept out there. After he wiped it clean, he grabbed the ice tray from his freezer and emptied it into the bottom of the cooler before placing the food he had on top of it. They'd need to get some other things, but it was a good start. Snacks on the beach made everyone happy.

Since there wasn't a real plan other than the excursion

itself, Donovan decided to grab a tote bag he'd received at a veterinary conference in Ohio and shoved a blanket and a couple of beach towels in it. Glancing around the house to see what he might have missed, he spotted a bottle of his favorite wine on the rack, and grabbed that as well. It wasn't supposed to be chilled, pinot noir was meant to be drank at room temperature, but the sun would make it hot, so he tossed it in the cooler, and grabbed a couple of plastic wine glasses he had for using outside.

I think that's everything. Now let's go get the girl.

EVEN THOUGH HE was certain she wanted to spend the day with him, Donovan's nerves were at an all-time high of frenetic energy. He was practically buzzing, running over how to greet her, what to say, and how to act. *Just be yourself. No, wait. Don't do that. You're trying to win the girl. For more than the day.* The quick trip to her house didn't allow him any more time to overthink the situation, so he pulled into the arched driveway and rounded toward the front door. Expecting to go in, he was surprised to see Riley coming out of the house as he put the car in park.

As adorable as ever, she had on short denim shorts, Converse sneakers, what looked like a white t-shirt, and she was wearing his hoodie. *My hoodie.* The butterflies he had in his stomach fluttered en masse to his chest, nearly giving him a stroke. She was fucking adorable. Her long hair was piled up in a bun, and she had on plastic sunglasses that she definitely didn't buy with her new money. He hopped out of the car quickly to open the door for her as she jogged toward the SUV.

"Morning!" she said with a bright smile.

"Good morning," he replied, incapable of speaking any other words.

"So, tell me more about what we're doing today?" she asked as she hopped in the passenger seat.

"It's a surprise," he replied, still standing next to her holding onto her door.

"Well, what are you waiting for? Let's go," she said with a laugh, clearly waiting for him to shut the car door and get in on his side.

Smirking, Donovan couldn't help himself. "I believe we had an arrangement?"

"An arrangement?" she asked, sounding completely confused.

Donovan tapped his lips with his index finger and leaned toward her. Sitting in the large SUV, she was slightly above him. "Ohh, you want kisses? Already?" She laughed at his expectant gaze.

"Actually, I want them still. I never stopped wanting them," he replied, still smirking. He watched her blush, speechless and still. "So, pay up."

"Well, we did have an agreement." She grinned as she leaned down toward him, planting her lips softly to his in a sweet kiss. As much as he wanted to pick up where they'd left off the night before, the thought stirring him, he knew that the decent guy needed to take the sweet girl out for the day as promised.

"Thank you very much, milady. Now we can go. Watch yourself," he said as he shut the door between them and jogged around to his side. He could see her grinning as he passed by the front window, and if he could have high-fived himself ever in his life, it was in that moment.

. . .

RILEY AND DONOVAN spent the twenty-minute car ride talking idly, while he pointed out some of the homes of the rich or famous that he knew of as well as a few landmarks along the way.

"How is Scrappy doing?" he asked.

"Well, today, he ate all of the flowers that Bernard planted on the back deck. After he ate his breakfast," she replied. "He's a menace."

Unable to contain his laughter, Donovan asked, "Are you feeding him enough?"

A confused look spread across her face. "Fuck. I don't know. I think Bernard puts his food out and I give him some treats and shit so he'll like me. Sometimes I feed him. We're not on a schedule," she admitted, embarrassed.

"How much kibble is he getting?"

"Uh, like, six cups a day, maybe?"

Donovan laughed again. "Babe, the dog is fucking hungry. He should be eating like ten cups of food a day. He's almost full-grown. He's what, like, ten months old now?"

Riley's hands flew to her face as she gasped. "Oh my God. We aren't feeding him enough? What the fuck is wrong with me? I've been starving him?" She was way more upset than Donovan expected, hiding her face.

"Relax, it's okay. Just give him some more, starting tonight when you get home. He's not starving to death, he's just not full. And with the amount of energy he has, he's probably burning it all off at a record pace. He'll be fine. I promise." Donovan reached across the console and took her hand while steering with the other. Bringing her hand to his lips, he planted a small kiss and set it down on his lap, covering it with his larger one. "I swear, he'll be okay. Feeding him more might not stop him from eating the plants anyway, he *is* kind of a menace." He laughed, hard, making Riley snatch her hand back, which she promptly smacked his arm with.

"Donovan! That's not funny. I can call him a menace. He's mine. But you can't," she said, pursing her lips at him.

"Oh? Is someone getting attached to the big lug?" he said teasingly.

Riley turned away, folding her arms like a petulant child who'd been caught doing something their parents wanted them to do anyway. "Shut up."

"You know, it's okay to like the dog. He *is* yours, after all."

"Yeah, yeah," she replied. "I like him enough."

Donovan chuckled again. "You didn't grow up with animals, did you?"

Spinning her head toward him, she replied, her voice dripping with sarcasm, "What gave that away? The fact that I am starving my dog to death?"

"Yeah, mostly that." He grinned, unable to contain the booming laughter that followed. "I swear he'll be all right, Riley. Why don't you text Bernard and tell him to give Scrappy some more food? I'm sure that'll make you feel better." Donovan tried to say it sweetly, but he simply couldn't help the laughter that continued coming.

"Oh my God, Donovan. It's not *that* funny." She smacked his arm again playfully, and pulled her phone out, sending a message to Bernard.

"We're here!" he exclaimed, moments later.

As they pulled into a parking space laid out right against the sand, the massive beach before them, Riley looked up from her phone, a huge grin on her face.

"Wow," she muttered.

"Pretty nice, right?" Donovan was pleased with himself.

He knew it was going to be a good day. Perfect day. Perfect weather. Perfect girl.

What more could a nice-guy-in-training ask for?

Riley hopped out of the car before he could get the door for her and made her way to the edge of the parking lot, which was covered in sand that had blown inland. A cool breeze was just enough to offset the hot sun and she pulled his sweatshirt off, tying it around her waist. Turning to him, she asked, "So, what did you want to do?"

Her smile was calming. As nervous as he'd been about what to say, and what to do, her presence was relaxing. He could've done nothing at all with her and been perfectly content. But he needed to sell her on the Port, and fast.

"Let's check out the shops and then head out to the beach? I need to pick up a permit anyway."

"A permit for what?" she asked.

"For driving on the beach." He chuckled.

"Wait, what? You can drive... on the beach!" she exclaimed.

"Fuck, you are so cute," he said. Realizing what he'd done, he added, "I said that out loud, didn't I?"

Grinning, she replied, "Yes, you did."

Donovan pulled her to him, wrapping his arms around her. Leaning down, he kissed the top of her head. "Well, you *are* fucking cute. Now, let's go."

CHAPTER 16

RILEY

If memory served her, the way that Donovan acted—the way they acted *together*—was exactly what couples did. Riley had forgotten all about the fact that she wasn't feeding her beast of a dog enough food, she didn't think once about the secrets being kept in the house she inherited. What she did was enjoy herself. Without regret, not a care in the world, she gave in to the butterflies, the tender kisses, the strong arms wrapped around her as they watched the sun set. It was becoming something they did together, watching the sunset. Riley even let herself believe that it was an activity they could keep doing, night after night.

At first, her self-conscious discomfort with attention kept her from flirting with him, but soon after he planted the first kiss of the day to her lips, she forgot all about how terrible she'd been in past relationships, or that there weren't that many to speak of in the first place. None of it mattered after just a few moments with Donovan. She grinned, thinking of how she'd misjudged him when she first met him at the bar. Only a week earlier, who'd have thought they'd be stealing kisses on the beach, holding hands as they walked along the water, and sharing stories of their childhood. Certainly not her.

When it was time to go home, it was evident that neither of them wanted to leave, but they both knew that playing hookie again wasn't feasible. Donovan walked her to the door when they arrived in front of the Prescott mansion.

"Can I see you tomorrow?" he asked, caressing her face.

"Don't you have to see actual patients?" she replied, grinning.

"I do." He sighed. "It's going to be extra busy too since we rescheduled everyone."

"Was it worth it?" she fished for the compliment.

"Are you fucking kidding me?" He kissed her quickly before continuing. "I haven't had such a wonderful day in as long as I can remember." He kissed her again.

Every time his lips touched hers, she turned to putty. She now understood what it meant when people said they were weak in the knees. Grateful he was holding her and unsure she could even stand on her own when his lips touched hers, she pulled him closer.

Running his free hand up her back to the nape of her neck, he turned her head slightly, exposing her neck. A chill washed over her as he feathered kisses from her shoulder to her ear before taking her lips again in a passionate kiss, melting her into him. A small moan escaped as his tongue parted her lips and he deepened the kiss, pressing his body against hers.

"Do you want to come in?" she whispered.

"I think you know the answer to that," he replied, sighing.

"But you can't?" she asked, disappointed. All thoughts of chastity had long since vanished once he kissed her like that, but she sensed his hesitation.

"I need to get home to the dogs. And the cats. And, I have an early morning. Tomorrow is surgery day, so I'll be operating all morning before seeing regular patients." He hugged her, resting his head on top of hers. Her disappointment forced a sigh even though she adored his love of animals.

"I should probably check on Scrappy," she finally conceded.

"Yeah, you better feed that dog," he said, letting out a laugh.

"Oh my God, Donovan! I can't believe you!" she exclaimed, feigning upset. "You're such a jerk." She shoved him away gently, grinning.

"Sorry, I couldn't help myself."

"Uh-huh, I'll get you back."

"I'm looking forward to it." He stepped back and ran a hand through his hair. "Tomorrow is kind of crazy, but can I call you?" he asked. A hopeful grin spread across his lips.

"Yes, of course." She was smitten. Standing with him in front of the giant house seemed like an out-of-body experience for her. They were so comfortable, and yet they hardly knew each other. In the moment though, Riley determined that it didn't matter. She enjoyed being with him and decided to let the feelings in. The racing heart, the nervous giggles, and that intense burning in her core when he kissed her… she relished in it.

"What do you have going on?"

Jerked away from the thoughts of her crush, Riley realized she'd lost a whole day investigating what Jameson's secrets were, and why he had that picture hidden in a locked drawer. She needed a plan to get Bernard out of the house so she could snoop in Jameson's room.

"I'm going to explore Jameson's house. There are a lot of things I need to look through here," she replied vaguely.

"You mean, *your* house," he corrected her.

She grinned. "Yes, *my* house. I don't think I could ever get used to saying that."

"You will. It'll just take some time, is all," he replied.

Time. But how much time do I have here in Port Henry?

Riley looked up at Donovan with a soft smile. "You better get going. Thank you for an amazing day," she said.

"I'll check in with you tomorrow, maybe we can grab dinner or something?" he asked.

"How about we plan to get together Saturday? Tomorrow is Friday, and I need to do some things here."

A disappointed scowl emerged on his face. "A whole day?"

"Oh, come on, Doctor, surely you had a life three days ago before I arrived," she teased.

"I don't like it, but I know you have a lot to do. This place probably takes some getting used to I'd imagine," he said.

"That it does," she replied with a chuckle.

"Okay, Saturday then. I work a half day. It's usually busy, but I'll make sure I'm done by noon and we can enjoy some of the day."

"You got yourself a date, sir," She grinned.

Donovan leaned in to kiss her again, lingering.

"I'll talk to you tomorrow," she said, pushing him away gently.

Groaning, he replied, "Okay, okay. Sleep well, Riley."

"You too," she replied.

Donovan backed away toward his Escalade, not taking his eyes off her until he was in the driver's seat. She stood outside, watching, waiting to wave goodbye, when he shooed his hand at her and mouthed the words "Go inside." She giggled and waved, then blew him a kiss before opening the door and stepping inside. Only then did he pull away.

Riley sighed deeply, considering everything that had happened in the last few days. Donovan, of course, was an unexpected surprise, but so was everything about Port Henry. It wasn't the bourgeois, awful place she thought it would be. In fact, that day alone she'd had the pleasure of meeting a local beekeeper and had the most wonderful honey, another shop owner who was an artist, and several other truly interesting and kind people. She considered for a moment what it might be like to stay there.

Would she continue seeing Donovan? Would things escalate between them? The flush of her face had her fanning herself as she walked up the stairs toward her bedroom. At thirty years old, it wasn't completely preposterous to think she may have met someone she could see a future with. But what did she know about him, really? She concocted a pros and cons list to seeing Donovan and by the time she reached the top of the stairs, there were far more pros than cons. But, she did realize she knew very little about him as a person. Sure, he was kind, and deliciously sexy, there was no denying that. She felt a little grin form as she thought about running her fingers along his toned torso.

Snap out of it. You need to get to the bottom of Jameson's secrets and get the fuck out of here. It's not your home. The angel on her shoulder told her one thing. But the little devil had a louder voice. *The hot doctor wants you, and you want him back. Get yourself some and have a good time before landing back in the city.* Neither voice told her to catch any real feelings, and she didn't plan to.

Riley walked into her room to find Scrappy sprawled

across the bed, his head on a pillow, snoring away. *He sure did make himself my sidekick.* As annoying as she found the dog at times, she also found him sweet. He didn't bark much and when she was home—or, in the house—he was with with her constantly.

She got ready for bed and scooted him over. Riley rubbed Scrappy's head absentmindedly, while thinking about how to get Bernard out of the house so she could freely go through Jameson's room without answering any questions. As much as she didn't want to admit it, having the dog lay next to her wasn't terrible. In fact, it was rather peaceful, even if he did take up a good portion of the bed when he stretched out. She ran her fingertips over his giant head, gently tugging on his soft ears as he sighed, and wondered if he missed Jameson. He seemed like a happy-go-lucky dog and for as much as she knew about dogs, which wasn't much, he didn't seem depressed or anything. She decided to ask Donovan when she saw him.

I'm becoming one of those weird obsessed dog owners already. And I don't even think I'm keeping him. She leaned down and rested her head on Scrappy's neck, a little flutter in her heart vibrating when she thought of giving him away. *But I can't keep him. I live in the city.*

"It's what's best for you, buddy," she whispered to him as she closed her eyes and drifted off to sleep, spooning the canine who was none the wiser to her plans.

THE NEXT MORNING, Riley woke up not having slept well and dreading her plan to snoop more than she would've liked to admit. Without any plan, she had no idea how to get Bernard out of the house and not raise suspicion. Briefly, she considered just telling him what she found and what she was looking for, but thought better of it after a couple of days. Bernard had no loyalty to her, his allegiance had been to Jameson, and while she didn't fault him for it, she didn't totally trust him either.

Scrappy was already awake, lying on the floor, staring at her. "What's up, Scrappy?" she said to him. He just tilted his head back and forth and stood up, wagging his tail. "You wanna get some breakfast?"

He started to whine a little, and dance in place. That's what she called it. His "puppy dance." Scrappy would perform tiny little jumps in place if he heard something he liked. He definitely liked the idea of breakfast, so Riley pulled herself out of bed to accommodate her hungry dog.

As he had been every morning that she stayed there, Bernard was in the kitchen, reading a book and drinking coffee.

"Morning, Riley. Sleep well?" he asked her.

"Not especially," she replied.

"I'm sorry. Is there anything I can do to make you more comfortable?"

A pang of guilt hit her. Bernard was a nice man. And she wasn't normally a liar. But she had to stick to her plan.

"I don't think so, but thank you for asking," she replied. "I was wondering if you could go to the grocery store and get a few things that I need today?"

"Of course, Riley, just make me a list and I'll head over there this afternoon." He moved to the coffee pot and poured her a cup. "Did you have a nice time with the doctor yesterday?"

She felt herself blush a little and couldn't suppress the grin coming on. "We did have a nice time. We went down to the far end of town where you can drive on the beach. Are you familiar?" she asked.

"I am indeed. Perfect time to go. The summer folks are going to start showing up this week, and some of those areas that aren't private are going to get pretty crowded."

"That's what Donovan said," she replied, then remembered what he had also said about Scrappy's diet. "Oh, he also mentioned that we're not feeding Scrappy enough. He should be eating like, ten cups of food a day, so would you mind picking some more up while you're out today?"

"Wow, ten cups? I guess I shouldn't be surprised. He is a big boy," he replied with a laugh. "I will add that to the list."

"Thanks, Bernard."

"You're welcome. So what do you have planned for today?" he asked her.

Riley's heart started beating a little harder, her guilt thumping in her chest. "I was planning to begin sorting out Jameson's things. If this is going to be my house, then I suppose I should know everything that's in it, don't you think?" She expected Bernard to raise an eyebrow or give some hint that he didn't want her going through certain things, something that would give away what happened to the photo, but he was as even-keeled as ever.

"I think that's a grand idea. In fact, I'm sure that Mr. Prescott would have wanted you to make whatever changes you thought would make it more like your own home."

He gave her nothing. Not even a sideways glance. Riley sighed quietly, drinking her coffee and writing out a random grocery list she thought might keep Bernard out of the house long enough for her to quickly root through Jameson's room. Once she handed it off, she excused herself to shower and change, Scrappy in tow as usual, and waited for Bernard to leave.

Once she was sure he was out of the driveway and on his way into town, she raced across the hall to Jameson's room.

CHAPTER 17

DONOVAN

Every Friday, Donovan spent the first half of the morning doing pro bono surgeries and the afternoon performing other procedures. One after another. Part of a veterinarian's job—well, any good veterinarian that cared about the community—was participation in the trap, neuter, release program for free-roaming cats. They weren't called strays anymore, it wasn't politically correct, and it implied that nobody cared about them. Feral wasn't used either, as it made people think of wild beasts, so the term free-roaming had become the new norm. Donovan would neuter or spay about five to ten cats every Friday that were trapped by volunteers of the local cat rescue, who then ensured the cats were nursed back to health and returned to where they came from.

Cat colonies were a problem in most cities, and Port Henry was no different. Donovan was happy to help, as the shelters couldn't keep up with the number of kittens born each year to the free-roamers, so the TNR program helped keep those numbers lower, year over year.

In addition to his work with the cat rescue, Donovan performed whatever non-emergency surgeries were needed by his patients, or any procedures that required the animal to be put under anesthesia. After he spayed four cats, a light week, he moved on to Anastasia Meowington, a fifteen-year-old Persian cat who needed her teeth scraped. That was not a procedure anyone wanted, nor could they do on a cat, without anesthesia.

After Ms. Meowington, was Reginald Beau Dacious, a German shepard that had developed hip dysplasia. A more complicated an unusual surgery, hip replacement on a German Shepard took a while to complete. Normally, for such a long surgery, Donovan would have sent the owner and pup to a larger animal hospital, but Mr. Davenport had been friends with his mom for many years. As he hummed along to the music Toni had chosen for the morning, he made a note to call his mom and make dinner plans. She had retired about five years prior, at Donovan's insistence, and they usually got together once a week or so for dinner or lunch. He'd been so distracted by Riley's hurricane rolling into town that he'd not been in touch with her for a few days.

"What are you so chipper about? Have fun playing hookie?" Toni asked, eyeballing him over her surgical mask.

"Who me?"

"No, I'm asking the dog. Of course you," she replied sarcastically. "What's going on with you and the new girl?"

"She has a name," he said.

"Oh, you care about this one's name. Must be serious," she teased.

Donovan raised a gloved hand, forceps still in the other, and flipped her the middle finger. "I actually like her, Toni."

"Interesting."

"Why is that interesting?" he replied, going back in to finish up the hip replacement.

"Because you tend to go for the emotionally unavailable. So, what's her story?"

Donovan just glared at her, disinterested in being teased about the feelings he was already developing for Riley. It was bad enough he had no idea what he was doing; he didn't need Toni making him feel like a jackass.

"Okay, I'm sorry, Doc. I can see that I've struck a nerve. Seriously though, what's her story?"

Donovan thought about what he was ready to share. He and Toni were close, but they didn't tend to discuss their personal lives in great detail. But he did want to sing praises of Riley, and didn't really have anyone else to tell.

Not raising his head from his work, he said, "I took her out to the edge of the island yesterday. She's not totally sold on Port Henry and I'd like to see her stay."

"What doesn't she like about the Port? Not enough hustle and bustle, like the city?" she asked.

"I think it's mostly that she landed here without any plan. She didn't know that Jameson was sick—none of us did, really—and she definitely didn't expect to inherit everything he had."

"Like that dog." Toni laughed.

"Exactly," he said with a chuckle.

"So, did you sell her on it?"

"I think so, but I don't know. She keeps some things close to the vest," he replied sincerely. "She's very sweet, and funny. She makes me laugh."

"And she's smoking hot," Toni added.

"She is that," Donovan agreed.

They both chuckled as Donovan sewed up the last few stitches on Reginald. "So are you going to see her again? Are you *dating*?" she asked.

"I'd like to be?" he replied with a question.

"Donovan Hunter. You really like her!" Toni exclaimed, handing a small tin over the dog for him to toss his instruments in.

"Let's get him moved into his kennel, and then we can call Mr. Davenport."

"You're avoiding," Toni said sternly, taking off her mask.

Donovan removed his mask as well. "Yes, okay? I like her. I totally dig her. She doesn't fall at my feet, she wants absolutely nothing from me but my company, and she makes me smile. And when we kiss—"

"You kissed her?" Toni's eyes grew wide. "Tell. Me. More!" she demanded.

"Oh my God, woman, you're ridiculous," he replied.

"No, I'm serious. I'm watching you talk about her, and you've never talked about anyone like this before. It's a sight. I should go get my phone. You have puppy dog eyes. The world should see this," she teased, pretending to leave the room. "Although, the sexy doe eyes thing is gonna go viral, then we're gonna be up to our eyeballs more than we are, in rich, socialite dog owners rubbing their fake tits on you. We can't have that." She was laughing full-on, clearly amused with herself.

"Are you done?" he asked.

Still laughing, she replied, "No, not yet. I need to experience more of the complete embarrassment I see all over your face." She winked at him.

"Fuck off, Antoinette," he said.

"Oh, using my full snooty name? You must really like her.

This is just too delicious for words." she kept the teasing going as long as she could.

"You're fired," he said.

"Until Monday, when you need an assistant again," she replied. "You know you don't want to go through the trouble of hiring and training someone new. You're stuck with me, Doc."

Giving in to the joke, he conceded, "You're right. But I'm happy to be stuck with you."

"Wow, you really are going soft," she said, giggling audibly as she left the room.

Quietly mocking her laughter so she wouldn't hear him, he took the dog to the kennel. After settling Reginald in his bed, he heard the jingle of the doorbell. Before he could ask who it was, Gavin walked in.

"What's up, Doc?" he asked, laughing at his own joke. "Get it? What's up, Doc?"

"I got it the first four hundred and twelve times you've said it since I became a vet. What brings you by this afternoon?" he asked, a little skeptical about what his answer might be.

"It's Friday afternoon, brother, let's go have some drinks!" he said.

Donovan briefly considered what his plans were and realized he had none because Riley had things to do, so he agreed. Gavin was trouble, but nothing that he couldn't handle. They'd been friends forever, and there was no reason why he shouldn't. Except the voice in his head reminding him that if annual plans were to be any indication of what Gavin had in mind, he'd want to pick up women and Donovan did not want to do that. Not by any stretch, and as he thought about Riley, he realized they hadn't spoken all day and he needed to get in touch, to see how things were going. The little angel on his shoulder was no match for Gavin's ever persuasive and well-prepared speech regarding the need for men to get out and stretch their legs and socialize with other men.

Since he'd already agreed before Gavin had even finished talking—mostly to himself—Donovan finished up some of his paperwork before calling it a day, while Gavin hung around the office, to Toni's dismay. Gavin had left a particularly sour impression on Toni when shortly after her divorce, he tried to date her, while he was her real estate agent, a total professional faux pas by any stretch of the imagination. Also, it wasn't a date he was looking for so much as a good time which Toni wasn't even remotely interested in. They'd run into each other at the Rusty Scupper one night while Donovan was otherwise occupied, and in Toni's words, "that lech of a friend" tried to get her to leave with him, when he'd already set up a tryst with some other woman. When he'd discovered his mix-up, he suggested that the three of them head back to his place for a good time.

To Donovan's surprise, the other woman, who was not only married, but well-known around town as happily so, was all for it. Toni, on the other hand, was not. She wasn't looking for a new husband, but she sure wasn't looking for a threesome either. Donovan didn't think Gavin was serious about it, nor did he think that Gavin would even know what to do with two women at once, but it happened nonetheless. Even though Toni wouldn't give him the time of day then, or ever, it didn't stop him from flirting with her shamelessly when he came by to see Donovan.

Reginald had been the last surgery of the day and Toni agreed to wait for Mr. Davenport to come pick up the dog. It wouldn't be long anyway; he lived less than a mile away, which was the only reason he didn't stay in the waiting room during the surgery. Also why Donovan let him take the dog earlier than he would normally. The office and his home were close enough to Mr. Davenport's that if there were any complications, he could be there quickly.

Toni gave Gavin an eye roll as he bid her goodbye and gifted him a stern "I'm watching you" look, pointed fingers and all. *All right, Mom, I'll stay out of trouble.* He responded with what he hoped came off as a "What? I didn't do anything wrong" shrug. And he didn't intend to do anything wrong. Not that things with Riley were official, he didn't even know what they were, but he hoped for them to be something more than nothing. And that was good enough for him to behave himself, besides the fact she was the only thing on his mind anyway.

They decided to go to the Nautical Mile, a martini bar a few miles away. Donovan sent Riley a text, just asking how her day was, and put his phone away. *She said she was busy, so don't harass her. You gotta play it cool.*

Playing it cool was something Donovan thought he'd been extremely good at, but as he checked his phone countless times, his preoccupation became evident to his friend.

"What's going on with you tonight, dude?" Gavin asked.

"Who me? Nothing, why?" Donovan innocuously took a sip of his bourbon. Not much of a martini guy, he preferred the amber liquid to most other alcohol.

"You've checked your phone like, eleventy billion times. Who are you waiting to hear from? And since when are you *that* guy?"

Pursing his lips into a sneer, he countered, "What guy is that, exactly?"

"The guy that waits for a woman to respond to him. *That guy.*" Gavin called him out, waiting for a response, but

Donovan was without words. Not wanting to jinx what was happening with Riley, even though she wasn't responding, he also didn't want to hear Gavin's smarmy two cents on the topic.

"I don't know what you're talking about. It's been a long week, I've just been checking the time. I'm exhausted," was the excuse he settled on.

"Whatever dude, I know you're lying. I've known you since we were kids. You're not fooling anyone. But if you wanna have your secret, you go right ahead." Gavin nodded in the direction of a group of ladies that had gathered at the other end of the bar, all sipping Cosmopolitans. The overdone makeup, short shorts, and what appeared to be fresh botox on each of the three girls gave them away as new. They'd just arrived from the city to start their summer early. Young, probably mid-twenties, this was likely their first expensive vacation and they appeared to be on the hunt as much as Gavin was.

"All you, bro," Donovan said.

"There's enough for both of us, and even an extra," he said with a laugh.

Growing agitation had settled in his stomach and he couldn't decide whether to be annoyed he hadn't yet heard back from Riley, or be concerned. Then, he wondered if he was supposed to care at all.

"I'm gonna pass tonight, bro, but I'll be here waiting with your drink when they reject you," Donovan teased him, grinning, and raised his drink to his buddy.

"You're a dick," he replied. "I'll be back."

Donovan pulled his phone out again.

Zero new messages.

CHAPTER 18

RILEY

With an outstretched hand, Riley touched the gold doorknob to Jameson's room. Looking down at Scrappy, who was by her side, she said, "Sorry, buddy, you can't go in there with me." He whined at her, as if he understood he'd be left outside the door to keep watch.

Suddenly, her eagerness to find out what was inside had waned and anxiety, in the form of nausea and fluttering in her chest, had replaced it. *It's my house. I can go anywhere I want.* She knew that was true, but it didn't take away from the feeling she was doing something she shouldn't. Sucking in a breath, she turned the knob quickly and walked inside the room, shutting the door behind her just as fast as she'd opened it.

At first glance, the breathtaking view from the floor-to-ceiling windows across the far side of the room caught her attention. A picturesque panorama of the beach, far beyond the property of the home, was visible, the bluish water offset by the sandy beach. The room was much larger than Riley expected; in fact, the giant king-sized bed positioned near the windows was dwarfed by the open space surrounding it. Dark wood floor panels contrasted the rest of the room, particularly the bed.

Completely made up in white linens with a white comforter, white throw pillows, and a white and oak headboard, it looked like it had been made up and staged for a magazine shoot. The entire area was minimalist and modern, with almost no personal touches, except for the large dog bed on the floor next to the window as well. Small oak nightstands, with matching sleek silver lamps placed upon them were symmetrically set on either side of the bed, made up the remainder of the furniture on that side of the suite.

Cautiously taking a step further inside the room, Riley caught a glimpse of the master bathroom to the left, and what appeared to be the closet off to the right of the room. A long dresser with shiny white lacquer stretched along the wall where she was standing near the door. She decided to start there.

She gently ran her hand along the top of the glistening dresser, which had no handles. It reminded her of old furniture, the type from the fifties that had little V-shaped stands and shiny knobs. Once she figured out that the drawers had a small indentation to pull, she slowly dragged the first drawer open.

Empty.

She yanked open the next drawer, finding the same. Not a stitch of clothing. No personal effects. Nothing. Drawer after drawer, she quickly realized the entire dresser had been cleaned out. Racing across the room, she threw open the closed door she presumed was to the closet and flipped on the lightswitch. Empty hangers swung from the force of the door as she rushed inside the walk-in closet.

What the fuck.

As she got deeper into the closet, she spotted a small box high upon a shelf. Resembling an old hat box but much smaller, the round container appeared to have been intentionally hidden away. Riley glanced around, looking for a way to climb up. Before she could leave the closet to get a chair or something else to stand on, she heard the door open, and Scrappy came running directly to her.

"What are you doing in here?" Bernard asked, his voice booming through the empty closet. His furrowed brows and pursed lips demonstrated his agitation with what he found before him.

"I'm looking for something," she replied nonspecifically. Her heart, now in her throat, was thumping hard enough she was sure she could hear it echo in the closet as it was in her ears.

"What would that be?" he asked.

His stern demeanor once again made Riley feel like she was trespassing, but he and the lawyer had made it very clear she was to consider this her home. She didn't owe him an explanation yet she couldn't help but attempt to find a reasonable excuse for her snooping.

She swallowed her fear and placed her hands on her hips for support. "You know, I don't owe you an explanation. This is *my* house." The words, bitter on her tongue, made her cringe inside. Riley didn't want to be mean to Bernard, but she wasn't ready to explain herself, and he could have been more forthcoming with her instead of letting her roam around looking for things. Besides, nobody else had been in that house that she was aware of, so he knew more than he was letting on.

"You're right, Riley. It is. Carry on," he said, before turning to walk away.

That's it? Carry on? Whatever, I'm getting that box down.

After rummaging through the rest of the suite, Riley found a small step stool in the bathroom, which provided just enough height for her to grab the box in the closet. As it fell into her hands, the weight indicated it didn't have much inside. Crouching to her knees, she set the box on the step stool and stared at its dust-covered exterior. Innocent enough looking, with its kraft brown outer shell, it also had a thin burlap ribbon holding the lid down.

She gently plucked at the bow, allowing the ribbon to fall to the sides of the box before she gently lifted the lid to inspect the contents.

To her dismay, the box contained an envelope filled with hundred dollar bills. Ten of them. A thousand dollars. There was nothing else inside the box. She'd snapped at Bernard over a handful of cash she didn't even need.

Disappointed in her own behavior, Riley shrank into a ball, curling up in the middle of the closet, wrapping her arms around her legs and resting her head on her knees. Her heart ached for answers, which she was beginning to realize she'd never find without help. Sadness washed over her as she concluded that none of the things in that room were of Jameson's choosing. The room had been whitewashed, removed of anything that could be sentimental or stand as reminders of the former occupant.

She laid down, staring at the ceiling of the closet, considering how she found herself there in the first place. No longer did she believe it was a coincidence that Jameson Prescott found his way into her life, but there were no clues pointing to why. Scrappy joined her in the closet and sprawled out next to her, cuddling his large body against her. As she stroked his soft fur, he sighed and started to fall asleep. Not long after, on the floor of the empty closet, Riley found herself dozing off, likely from the adrenaline crash or the stress of all the changes.

SEVERAL HOURS LATER, Riley woke up without a clue where she was. Startled at first, she shot upright, scaring Scrappy who let out a small growl. He'd been asleep right next to her.

"Sorry, boy," she soothed him. "I forgot where I was for a minute."

Scrappy huffed, the way only a big dog can, as if he didn't want to hear it. His nap had been interrupted and he clearly wasn't ready to get up.

Unsure of what time it was, Riley yawned and got up, stretching before walking out of the closet, back into Jameson's bedroom. Scrappy followed her lead, performing the downward dog and yawning before his tail began to wag. He watched Riley, anticipating her next move. She picked the box back up and inhaled a sharp breath.

"Scrappy, it's time to get some answers," she said. He did his usual hop in place, waiting for her to move so he could follow.

They traipsed down the stairs, each step a chore as Riley considered what she would say to Bernard. She wasn't sure where he was but didn't have to look far. He was sitting in the kitchen at the bar, sipping something amber out of a rocks glass. *Yeah, I could use a drink too.*

He noticed her right away and raised his glass. "Would you like one?" he asked.

Nodding, she replied, "Yes, please."

"You got it."

Bernard got up and walked to the counter where the bottle of whiskey was sitting and grabbed a glass for her out of the cabinet. A small, silver ice bucket was sitting on the counter next to the bottle. He tossed two ice cubes into the glass and poured a solid three fingers over top. Riley couldn't help but grin, that was a lot of whiskey, but she also needed something to take the edge off the conversation and it seemed Bernard knew it.

He walked back with the full glass and set it down in front of her. "I'm guessing you have questions about something?" he said.

She nodded silently and took a sip of her drink. As the liquid hit her throat, the warm sensation trailed all the way to her empty stomach.

"What would you like to know, Riley?" Bernarnd asked, in a soft and tired voice.

She blew a breath out, letting the air cool her mouth from the spice of the whiskey. "Well, first of all, Jameson just died, did he not? Why is his room empty?"

"It was part of his instructions to me upon his passing."

"Where did his things go?" she asked.

"Most of it was donated. There are a few personal effects in the attic, which you can see whenever you like."

She paused, deliberating internally what to ask next. "Why did he want his room cleaned out?"

"I'm not entirely sure, to be honest with you, but I suspect that he didn't want you to get so attached to his things that you wouldn't move into that room yourself," he replied.

"You think he wanted me to move in there? Why?"

"Because, as you mentioned, it is your house. He wanted you to be comfortable here, that much I know for certain."

"What's with the box of money?" she said, tapping the lid of the box in front of her.

"It was in the closet. Probably an emergency pile of it." Bernard shrugged.

"Was that normal for him?" she asked.

"Yes. There's money stashed all over this house. Jameson thought he needed to be prepared, just in case."

"Just in case what?"

Bernard laughed. "I don't know, exactly. I guess an emergency where he couldn't get access to cash?"

Riley smiled. She wanted more answers though, and didn't want to let the rapport she and Bernard had impair her judgement. "Look, there's something you're not telling me, Bernard. We both know it."

His smile disappeared as his brows drew in tight together. Riley stared at him blankly, waiting for something—anything —that would shed some light on what the hell was going on. He took in a deep breath and let it out hesitantly. "What would you like to know, Riley?" he asked again.

"I don't know! That's the problem, Bernard," she exclaimed, completely exasperated.

The knowing expression on Bernard's face was clear, he did know something, but he wasn't going to make it easy. He stood up abruptly, causing Riley to jump a bit.

"Riley, Jameson Prescott and I were friends for thirty years. He was my friend, and I intend to honor every one of his wishes. I know that this isn't easy for you." Both stern and sympathetic, he continued. "If there is something specific you want to know, ask me. I will do my best to answer your questions. But in the meantime, this is your house, and all the answers you're looking for are here. That much I know."

Not waiting for a reply, Bernard drained his glass and set it in the sink on his way out of the room.

CHAPTER 19

DONOVAN

The rest of the evening with Gavin had been uneventful. Eventually, Donovan stopped checking his phone incessantly and enjoyed his friend's company. Once Gavin struck out with the ladies at the other end of the bar, the two moved to a small high top table to chat. Anxiety over Riley had cast a shadow on Donovan's mood, and he feared she changed her mind about him and was going dark. Against his better judgement, he mentioned to Gavin that they had gone out and had to listen to a tirade of remarks about how he was supposed to be a wingman, not get wrapped up in a girl before summer even got underway.

Donovan tried to play it off, not wanting to explain himself further to someone who clearly wouldn't understand. He decided he'd ask Toni for advice the next morning at work. She was always good for giving it to him straight. Well aware he could be overreacting, he didn't care—his heart and other organs ached for her, and he believed it to be reciprocal. Succumbing to romantic emotions was so far outside of Donovan's box, he felt lost. Toni would know what to do.

AFTER A RESTLESS NIGHT OF SLEEP, and fighting off the urge to call or text Riley a thousand times just to check in, he went to work with what could only be described as a sourpuss. Toni was busy getting the day's files out and didn't pay much attention to him until she sat down to organize something on her desk.

"Jesus Christ, Donovan," she said, eyes wide.

"That bad?" he asked.

"Uh, yeah. How much did you drink last night?" she asked.

"I hardly drank at all!" he exclaimed.

"Well, you look like shit. What the hell happened to you?"

"Nothing happened," he said, hesitation in his voice.

"Well, obviously something happened."

Donovan gave a sheepish half-smile.

"You wanna talk about it?" she asked, softening her tone.

Donovan nodded.

"Okay, after we take care of Margie's cat, we have a break. She'll be here any second now," Toni replied.

"What's wrong with her cat? Is it the cat or the new kitten?" Donovan asked, concern in his voice.

Margie Bremmerton had found a single newborn kitten on her patio about a month prior, barely breathing and with its little eyes still glued shut. Donovan had showed her how to bottle feed it, keep it warm, and how to stimulate it to go to the bathroom. Newborn kittens couldn't excrete without their moms help, so she had to do it since there was no mother cat to be found. Donovan suspected that the mother had thought the baby was already gone, but somehow they'd managed to save it. A newborn kitten was volatile at best though, and required constant care to ensure they made it.

"It's the kitten. She's just here for her first round of vaccines." Toni grinned.

"No way, she survived?" A feel-good outcome like that made Donovan's heart grow on the spot.

Just then, Margie walked in, a little kitten wrapped in a blanket in her arms. The black kitten's eyes were open, a sparkling bright green, and it was meowing a tiny cry.

"Margie! Who do we have here?" In two strides, he was at her side, taking the baby to hold himself. He loved baby animals just like any other person would, and he wanted to snuggle the little furball.

"Doc, this is Antonio. Turns out, he's a boy," she replied.

Donovan flipped the kitten over and nodded. "You are correct, it sure is." He turned his attention back to the kitty. "Come on, Antonio, let's get you some shots."

Toni waved Margie to follow Donovan as he took off down the hall, holding the kitten close with one hand. In the exam room, he set the kitten down on a small scale and made a note of the weight.

"Is he eating well?" Donovan asked.

"He is a piggie, actually," Margie replied with a laugh. She was a local resident, married to Mike Henderson, a guy Donovan had gone to high school with. They met in college and when Mike came back, he brought Margie with him. A nice couple, they didn't have any kids, and they worked with Donovan on the free-roaming cats program, helping trap and take care of them after their surgeries. She had tried to find the mother cat for some time, but they suspected either something happened to her, or she moved on to a new place.

"He does have a nice round belly," Donovan said, rubbing the kitten's stomach. "And he's so friendly. You've done an amazing job here. I gotta admit, I wasn't sure he'd make it."

"Well, if it wasn't for you teaching me how to bottle feed and everything, he might not have. Takes a village," she said with a chuckle.

"Ha! It sure does. Okay, well, let's get him some vaccines and schedule his neuter surgery, so we don't have any more little Antonio's running around, sound good?"

"Perfect," she replied.

Donovan grabbed the little guy's vaccines and in no time, they were on their way with an appointment to come back two weeks later.

AFTER THEY LEFT, Toni brought up their earlier conversation. "We have about an hour before we have three more patients back to back. Slow for a Saturday, thankfully for you. So, tell me what's going on," she said. "Did something happen with Riley?"

"Well, not really. And maybe I'm overreacting. But I feel like we have a connection."

"So, what happened?" she asked.

"The other night, you know I went out with her and we had an amazing time. Like seriously, it was incredible. We click, you know?"

Toni nodded, waving her hand for him to continue.

"So, I had asked her if we could see each other yesterday, but she said she had a lot to do at the house, but she wanted to. So we agreed to get together and do something today."

"I don't see the problem," Toni said.

"Well, the problem is that I haven't heard from her. I texted twice yesterday, but she never replied. Now, I am aware she said she was busy, but we did say we'd talk or text or something. So, I haven't heard from her since the night we went out, when I thought we had something." Donovan pouted, giving Toni the puppy dog eyes. He knew part of him was being obsessive but getting another opinion before he "what iffed" himself to death was imperative.

He expected her to laugh, but surprisingly, she reached out and touched his forearm gently. "Well, first, I'm sorry I teased you about her. You obviously really like her."

"I really do, Toni. You *know* me. Relationships? They're not really my thing, but everything about her has hit me like a ton of bricks. From her sass to her ass," he joked.

Toni laughed. "Yeah, well. You need to give her a little space. This whole relationship thing might be new and thrilling to you, but you gotta contain your excitement or you're gonna scare her off. She doesn't know this town, she just lost her friend, and as we have previously discussed, she just inherited a whole new life, to an extent. And that's a lot of change in a short period of time. That's the kind of thing that will make someone cut and run before you can blink an eye if you pressure them too much."

"So, give her space? That's your advice?" Donovan groaned.

"What did you think I was gonna say? Run over there like what's his name in *Say Anything* and hold a boombox over your head?" she asked sarcastically.

"So, no grand gesture, got it," he said with a slight chuckle.

"Yeah, I think you need to be cool. Give the girl a chance. If she said she had stuff to do at the house, who knows what she found or had to do. She could've had a real shit day and didn't wanna rub that juju all over you and whatever it is you have going on between ya," Toni suggested.

"That had not occurred to me," he replied.

"You have to work today, so we work, then you give her a call or swing by later. You already had some kind of tentative plans for today, did you not?"

"We did," he said.

"Well then, it's not outside the scope of reason for you to want to follow up on those plans. But don't be all possessive and weird about it. I'm sure she likes you. You're good-looking and likeable. And you love animals. That's probably the best thing about you," she said with a smirk.

"Are you hitting on me?" he teased her.

"And, now you can fuck off. Don't ruin your new relationship." She spun her chair around to get back on the computer.

"Thank you, Toni," he said, as he started to walk down the short hallway, back to his office for a bit before the next patient arrived.

"You're welcome, jackass," she replied.

Donovan considered what Toni said. She was completely right. In his attempt to be the nice guy, it had almost become some kind of obsessive overkill. He'd never felt that connected to a woman before and was afraid to lose it. But if giving it space to breathe or smothering it to death before the relationship got off the ground were his choices, he was going to be cool. *That's the theme for today. Just be cool.*

CHAPTER 20

RILEY

Riley sat in the kitchen, her jaw slack from surprise. "All the answers you're looking for are here." That's what Bernard said. *Except they fucking disappeared.* She'd already gone back through much of her notes and hadn't found anything that gave her pause, other than the obvious, that she lost her friend, and the book wasn't done. She still wasn't sure she was going to finish it. That may have been Jameson's final wish, or so she was told, but the thought of working on it without him made her too sad.

Feeling completely alone, she decided to call in reinforcements and picked up her phone.

"Hey! How are you?" Collette answered without saying hello.

"Girl, I'm all right, but I could really use your company. Can you get away?"

"To the city?" she asked.

"Actually, I'm in Port Henry." Riley realized things had happened so quickly, she hadn't told her best friend that Jameson had died, that she'd inherited a giant dog, or that she was now the owner of a giant beach house.

"What the hell are you doing there?" she asked.

"Umm… it's a long story…" Riley replied, unsure where to begin.

"Did your sugar daddy invite you up for the summer and you finally admit that you're having an affair with that old man?" she teased.

"Actually, he died," Riley blurted out.

Silence fell over the line between them.

"Fuck. Riley, I'm so sorry. I was just kidding. Are you okay?"

"Well, I've been better."

"Is there anything I can do?" Collette asked.

"I was hoping you could come visit me here. Is there any chance you can come tonight? I can send a car for you. It's only like, four hours or something," she practically begged.

"Send a car for me? Who the fuck are you?" She laughed.

"I have a lot to tell you," Riley replied. "Can you come?"

Collette rifled through some papers audibly. "I can come tonight, but I have to leave tomorrow afternoon. I'm not done with my paper. Okay?" Collette had gone back to college to get her Masters in Business Administration and as a full-time employee and a part-time student, she had a lot on her plate.

"Deal."

"You don't need to send a car, I can drive myself. I have a book I've been wanting to listen to, so this is perfect. I can kill two birds with one stone. I'll leave in like, a half hour, is that fast enough?"

"Collette, you have no idea how badly I need you. Thank you so much," Riley replied.

"That's what friends are for, girl. I'll see you soon, and I'll text if there's any change."

"Okay, see you soon," Riley said before hanging up.

SHE DECIDED that some space between her and Bernard would be good for the time being and some fresh air would do her some good. Plus, Scrappy hadn't been outside and he seemed a little rammy. He'd been pacing around, stopping every few minutes to look up at her with his big brown eyes.

"You wanna go for a walk, boy?" she asked.

Riley learned immediately that "walk" was a word Scrappy was very familiar with, as his usual little hops turned into giant hops and he started turning in circles in excitement.

She laughed. "Okay, okay. Let's get your leash."

As she looked for the leash, she decided to grab a sweatshirt as it was dusk and likely getting cooler. She ran up to her room and spotted Donovan's gray hoodie, the NYU logo in blue, sitting on her chair. Picking it up, she held it to her face, inhaling the scent of him.

"Shit," she said. "I didn't call him today." She threw the hoodie on over her head, ran back downstairs, and hooked a very excited Scrappy up to his leash, completely forgetting to check in with Donovan on her way out.

They walked the neighborhood for at least an hour before Scrappy stopped pulling her with him and began trotting next to her like a good dog. "We need to let you outside more, don't we?"

Riley mused at how Scrappy always seemed to look back at her like he was trying to respond. He was growing on her. The whole town was.

. . .

WHEN THEY RETURNED HOME, Scrappy had dinner waiting for him, courtesy of Bernard, and he lapped up about a gallon of water as well.

Bernard was in the kitchen, seemingly waiting for them. "Did you have a nice walk?" he asked.

"We did," Riley replied, trying to ignore the tension between them.

"Would you like some dinner?"

"No, thank you. I'm not really hungry," she said. "Oh, my best friend is coming tonight, she'll be here in a little bit to see me. Do we have sheets or anything for one of the guest rooms?"

"I can take care of that," he replied. His tone indicated nothing was wrong, no residual tension on his end. Completely even-keeled, like usual. "How long will she be staying?" he asked.

"She's just going to be here for the night," Riley replied. "Are you sure you don't mind preparing a room for her?" Even though it was his job, she remained uncomfortable being waited on and felt guilty that he was going to do the work of setting up a room for her unexpected guest.

Giving her a soft, welcoming smile, he replied, "Riley, it's my job. I don't mind one bit. I'll put her in the room next to yours." He started to walk away, then paused. "Have you considered moving into the master suite?"

Her eyes grew wide. She had not considered moving in there. It didn't seem right. "I'm fine where I am," was her reply.

"Well, Mr. Prescott would have wanted you to have the master. It's one of the reasons that he had me redecorate it and clean out his belongings so quickly."

"I don't think I'd be comfortable with that right now," she replied.

"I understand," he said. "Is there anything else I can do for you?".

Riley paused for a moment, thinking over how she wanted to apologize. "Bernard, I'm sorry for snapping at you earlier today."

"There's no need to apologize. This is new for both of us, and I was asked to look after you by someone I cared very deeply for. Jameson was my boss, but he was also my friend. I don't agree with how he has chosen to handle everything, but I agreed to respect his wishes. I hope you understand that," he said.

"I can't help but feel like there is something that I should know about him that you could be telling me, Bernard."

"That might be true, but it's not the right time," he replied.

"When is the right time? How long am I supposed to stay here not knowing?" she asked in a childlike, frustrated tone.

"As long as it takes," he replied. "Now, if you'll excuse me. I want to get the room ready before your friend arrives. I'll make some snacks and leave them in the kitchen for you two as well."

Knowing she wasn't going to get any more out of him that night, she conceded, simply thanking him and heading to her room to shower and change. Being dragged around the neighborhood by an oversized Great Dane puppy was a great way to get a bit sweaty.

BY THE TIME Riley had showered and changed, Donovan was on her mind and she made a note to get in touch with him when she wasn't so distracted. She put the hoodie back on after her shower, it was comforting and that's the feeling she was shooting for. Far too big for her, it felt like a cozy blanket. A devilish grin spread across her face as she recalled their moment on the beach when she made the first move.

Totally uncharacteristic of her, she almost audibly giggled thinking of how she was so compelled, it had to be done. She added that little tidbit to the growing list of things she needed to fill Collette in on.

ABOUT AN HOUR LATER, Collette was there. The total opposite of Riley in almost every way, she was boisterous, blonde, and loud. Relief struck Riley immediately upon hugging her best friend, as if she'd squeezed all the bad juju out.

"I know it's late, but can we light that fireplace outside and talk there?" she asked as she poked around, petting Scrappy the entire time. He was smitten with her right away, her energy and his completely in sync.

Before Riley could reply that she didn't know how to light the outdoor fireplace, Bernard jumped in. "Ms. Carter, why don't you head up to your room and get settled, and I'll get the fire going for you two," he suggested.

"That sounds amazing," she replied.

"Do you need help with your bag?" he asked.

"No, no. I'm good."

Riley and Colette headed up to her room, giggling like school girls. "You have a butler?" Collette whispered.

"He's not a butler," Riley hissed quietly.

"Uh, yeah he is." Collette laughed. "What the fuck is going on here, Riley?"

"I don't even know where to begin, girl," she replied.

"Well, let's start with whose NYU hoodie you're wearing and where is he?" Collette raised a suspicious eyebrow at Riley and smirked.

"Grab a sweatshirt, I'll fill you in on everything. Bernard is making snacks too," she added.

"Butler," Collette teased.

"He came with the house, shut up," Riley said.

"Did this giant dog with the sweetest face in the world come with the house too?" Collette leaned down to kiss Scrappy on his snout. "You're a big, goofy sweetheart, aren't you, boy?" she said to him in a baby voice.

"He did come with the house. Why? You want a dog?" Riley asked, offering her Scrappy half-heartedly.

"He loves you. He's yours now. I couldn't take him even if I wanted to."

"I can't keep him in the city, he's huge," Riley said.

"So, don't go back to the city." Collette said it so matter-of-factly, as if it were that easy.

"It's not that simple Collette," Riley began her excused.

"Um, we can discuss it further outside in front of your amazing, rich people *outdoor fireplace*, but yeah, it is that simple. You don't even have to fucking work. I mean, I know you, and you will, and that's cool and admirable and whatever, but why the fuck would you go back to the filthy city when you could live on the beach?"

Riley didn't have a good reply for that. The city was her home, it almost always had been, but spending time at the beach, even with all the confusion in her head and her heart, was refreshing. Maybe she had a point. So the girls headed outside with drinks and snacks, courtesy of Bernard, and Collette was filled in on everything that had happened.

CHAPTER 21

DONOVAN

The day was dragging on, but Donovan's mood had improved significantly after talking to Toni about things. Ruminating over their conversation, he ascertained that Toni was a better friend than he truly gave her credit for. With the brief time he had before patients came in, he decided to send Riley a quick, casual text, to say hello and ask if she was still free that evening. He had the next two days off and hoped they'd get to spend some more time together.

He recalled their earlier conversations, how easy it was for them to talk. Trying to convince her to stay in the Port had made him realize that he did love it there. For all of his past resentments of the affluent, he didn't hate it deep down, and couldn't really picture himself living anywhere else. They'd talked about her life in New York City, her apartment that overlooked Columbus Circle. He couldn't help but think she wasn't really happy there, even though she tried to convince him that the hustle and bustle was a life she loved.

Listening to her open up about her family, her divorced parents and absent father, it made sense to him why she had bonded with Jameson Prescott even though she didn't acknowledge it. She simplified their relationship by telling him that they simply connected and enjoyed chatting. That she enjoyed listening to him tell the stories of his global travels. What Donovan couldn't put his finger on was why Jameson befriended her specifically. He could have hired any writer in the world he wanted, to write his story. Why her?

Mid-thought, Toni knocked on the half opened door to his office.

"Hey, patients are here. And Mrs. Aldridge called about Bradley. She says the prednisone isn't working and wants to bring him in today."

Rolling his eyes, he asked, "Can we fit him in today?"

"Toward the end of the day, we can," she replied.

"Okay, let her know and we'll see what's going on."

He stood up and headed to Exam Room One to see his next patient. Grabbing the chart from the door before entering to see what was in store, he perused the intake form. "Ferret is vomiting and has diarrhea." *Awesome.*

Inside the exam room were a little boy and his mother, neither of whom Donovan had met before. A small ferret wearing a harness was in the little boy's arms.

"Hi there, I'm Dr. Hunter. Who do we have here?"

"This is Marcus. He's a ferret," the little boy answered before his mother jumped in.

"This thing has been throwing up and having terrible diarrhea for two days." She pointed to the animal is if it were contagious and she didn't want to catch whatever it had. Her well-manicured nails were a pale shade of pink, and her giant ring indicated she'd married well.

"Two days, you say?"

The little boy nodded.

"What's your name?" Donovan asked.

"Dylan," he replied.

"Mind if I take a look?" Donovan stretched out his arms to take the ferret, placing him on the exam table.

He palpated the little critter's belly, getting a hiss from him. "Okay, Marcus, I won't do that again." He soothed the animal with some head scratches and a few under the chin for good measure.

"Well, it doesn't feel like there's any obstructions. Has he been outside?"

"Yes, I let him out on his harness," the mom answered.

"Well, I'm pretty sure he ate something bad. Maybe a lizard or a bug that didn't agree with him. Has he been eating his food?"

"Not today. Yesterday he did, but then he started getting sick."

"Okay, I want you to put him on baby food for the next three days. Only chicken or some other meat though. Absolutely no fruit. And you can give him some scrambled eggs. Those will all be good for his tummy until whatever it is passes. He either ate something bad or has a bit of a stomach bug, but it doesn't seem to be serious."

"Baby food?" the mother asked.

"Yeah, human baby food is super high in protein, so it's good for ferrets. And the scrambled eggs are to entice him. They just like scrambled eggs and it won't agitate his stomach issues. If he doesn't eat those things, then give us a call and come back in, okay?"

Donovan handed Dylan the ferret after petting him again one more time.

"Thank you so much, Dr. Hunter. We were really worried," Dylan said.

"Yes, thank you, Doctor."

"You're welcome. If you'll wait outside for just a few minutes, Toni will take care of you."

HE FILLED Toni in on what was going on with the ferret and headed to his next two appointments, both already waiting for him.

FINALLY, the last few patients of the day, but first, the one he least looked forward to. Bradley, the Irish Setter, and Beverly Aldridge, again. Just a few days ago, she'd been in, pressing her tits against him as she walked by.

"She's waiting for you in Exam Room Two," Toni said. As Donovan took the file and walked toward the room, she grabbed his arm. "You might wanna keep the door open. Wait till you see." Toni shook her head in a "you'll never believe it" look.

Confused, Donovan shrugged and walked into the room. Immediately, he realized what Toni was referring to. He almost forgot there was a dog there at all when he laid eyes on Beverly. Not only was she wearing the shortest skirt he'd ever seen an adult wear, she had on a nude sheer, sweater blouse thing with a white bathing suit underneath. Innocuous enough, except that the white bathing suit was made of the thinnest material on the planet, and stretched against her enormous cleavage, was completely transparent.

Stunned in place, Donovan had to tear his eyes away from the nipples looking back at him and focus on the dog.

"Beverly." He cleared his throat. "What's going on with Bradley? *Seriously, what is she doing? Nobody could look away from that outfit. Just get through this exam.*

"Dr. Hunter, Bradley isn't doing any better," she said.

"He's still wheezing?" he asked.

"Yes, and he's very lethargic. Usually, he's larger than life," she said, stretching her arms out wide, as if making her tits a fucking billboard. The barely there material strained even harder as Beverly put herself on display.

Donovan bent down on one knee and placed his stethoscope in his ears, setting the diaphragm against Bradley's chest. As he listened, ignoring Beverly by averting his eyes, he could hear a bit of wheezing in the pup's lungs. Before he could stand, Beverly crouched down in front of him, almost exposing her vagina to him with her legs spread and her short shorts riding between her legs. Between the tits he couldn't help but continuing to accidentally look at, and her legs wide open in front of him, he didn't really know what to do with himself.

"What do you hear, Doctor?" she asked quietly.

Donovan stood up quickly, yanking the stethoscope from his ears. "Well… um…" He was having trouble gathering his thoughts, as all he could think of were the pert, round breasts and tight little nipples in front of him. Beverly was a living, breathing, walking temptation and while Donovan didn't particularly care for her, or what she was doing, he was still a man, and couldn't help the sexual attraction to the buffet in front of him. He had shut the door even though Toni had warned him not to, so before anything could happen, he opened it back up quickly, causing Beverly to step back as if she'd been caught doing something. "We're going to put him

153

on some antibiotics. It looks like maybe he caught a chest cold or something. But that should knock it right out of him."

Clearing his throat again, he stepped into the hallway, visibly uncomfortable, shifting his weight back and forth. Teetering on her high heels, Beverly followed him close behind.

"Toni, can you see if we have any of the antibiotic samples left for Bradley?" he asked.

She nodded and walked to the back room, leaving Donovan and Beverly out front alone with the dog. In the matter of a half second, Beverly stepped in close to Donovan, attempting to press her body into his. There were more patients coming at any moment, but Beverly had no shame. She came to get some Dr. Hunter, and she was going to make it clear what she wanted. Before Donovan could even push her away, she leaned in close and whispered, "My husband doesn't take care of me the way I know you could. Don't you like what you see?"

"Yeah, Dr. Hunter, do you like what you see?" a new voice asked as the front door jingled.

"Riley!" Donovan exclaimed, gently pushing Mrs. Aldridge away.

CHAPTER 22

RILEY

What in the actual fuck am I seeing right now? Riley walked into Donovan's office to surprise him, mostly to apologize for going missing the day prior. After a long chat with Collette, and some very best friend advice, she decided to tell him everything that was going on, and she felt like she owed him an apology in person, not in a text. But what she found was a forty-something-year-old woman in see-through clothing, whispering in his ear.

Without a word, she turned around and walked out. Donovan tried to follow her, calling out her name, but she kept walking back to her car. *Well, fuck him. It was one afternoon I blew him off and he's getting cozy with some other chick? I don't need it.*

Scrappy was waiting for her in the car, windows rolled down, of course. More than happy to have her back, he licked the side of her face from chin to eyebrow, leaving a trail of slimy dog drool in his wake.

"Come on, bro!" she snapped at the dog, wiping her face with her sleeve.

Riley turned on the car quickly and drove away, seeing that Donovan had gone back inside. Her heart sank at the humiliation and disappointment. She thought they had something special.

"Let's go on a little road trip, Scrappy. You ever been to New York City?" she said in her best fake, "let's get excited" voice.

Sure that Scrappy smiled back at her, she laughed, shook her head, and hopped on the freeway back to the city. She sent Bernard a text, letting him know she would be back in the morning, if not sooner, that she was picking up some stuff from her apartment, and he needn't worry.

The entire two-hour ride back, Riley expressed her deepest feelings to Scrappy. He'd hung out with her and Collette as they solved the world's problems, or at least the most recent of them, and since he didn't talk back, he made the best sounding board.

Scrappy seemed to listen intently as she poured her heart out about what she saw in Donovan's office, how she couldn't believe she thought they had a connection when he turned around and did such a thing. She recalled why she didn't date much in that moment.

BERNARD'S CONFESSION weighed on her as well. So, she discussed with Scrappy all the facts she had, racking her brain over what could possibly be the missing link between them. She thought back to when Jameson first hired her, and how she didn't particularly care how he'd found her, but now it seemed like much less a coincidence. That he'd sought her out for more than just her writing skills.

"I am a great writer, but I don't think that's the whole story," she said to him. "I wish you could talk, boy, I bet you know the whole story." Scrappy tilted his head, acknowledging her and she was sure that he did.

WHEN THEY GOT BACK to the city, they had managed to avoid most of the traffic, but finding parking was a real bitch, as it always was. She didn't have a car of her own, so she didn't have one of the fancy prepaid parking spots most city dwellers with cars did. Paying for parking wasn't really the issue, it was finding parking anywhere near her house. By the time they finally found a place to leave the car, she grabbed Scrappy's leash and walked him the two blocks back to her apartment.

It took far longer with him than it would have without him. Scrappy had to stop and sniff every single thing he happened upon, the least of which was other people. She found herself apologizing over and over for the friendly pooch as he licked, sniffed, and rubbed against just about every person they happened upon. Which, in New York City, was a lot.

Not lost on her was that she enjoyed his company. It had only been a short while that they'd been united, but he'd grown on her. From the very first moment, he'd become a loyal companion to her, sticking with her wherever she was. From her breakdown in the closet, to this very moment.

"I don't think I can let you go, boy," she whispered as they walked into her apartment. Just as she'd left it, the space seemed incredibly small, particularly when Scrappy started to wander, sniffing around.

She plopped on the couch, the two-hour drive and arduous walk catching up to her. She was still incredibly pissed off at Donovan, but moreso, the heat in her face was the humiliation she felt. It wasn't like her to get attached to someone, let alone a guy, and in such a short period of time.

"What was I thinking, dude?" She looked over at Scrappy, who'd finally settled on the couch next to her. *Ugh.*

Scrappy whined, then sighed. *Shit, I didn't bring him any food. I'm a horrible fucking dog parent. And I was already starving him.*

Palming her hand to her face, she pulled her phone out of her pocket. One great thing about the city was that you could have absolutely anything delivered. She found an app where she could order some dog food, then proceeded to order herself more Chinese food than any one person could possibly eat.

I'll eat my feelings and nap on it, she decided. The reason for heading back to the city was to pack up more of her belongings, some clothes, and other things she neede,d like a few of her books, but she decided to snuggle up with Scrappy while they waited for their dinner to arrive instead. *Manual labor can wait.*

The next thing she knew, there was a knock at the door.

CHAPTER 23

DONOVAN

Beverly left abruptly after Donovan tried to chase Riley down, huffing the way out to her car, leaving the dog's antibiotics behind. Toni assured Donovan she would take them over after they'd finished seeing patients and that he needed to see the last few before he addressed the Riley situation.

"You can't leave, you have patients here. There's only two, and they're not serious. Just take care of that, and I'll close up so you can go after her."

"I can only imagine what that looked like." He ran his hands through his hair nervously.

"It looked like you were in a precarious position with another woman," Toni replied.

"But I wasn't! I didn't do anything!"

"Calm down. I know that. But I did tell you to leave the door open."

"Uh, we were at the front fucking desk, Toni. How was I to know that she'd give zero fucks about hitting on me out in the open with her tits about to pop out?"

"All right, fair point. But I think it's time we deal with Beverly in a different way. No more seeing her alone, I'll be in the room with you at all times, deal?" she suggested.

"Sweet Jesus, yes please," he replied. "You know nothing has ever happened between us for her to think it's okay to act that way."

"I know. She's married. Not your type." Toni laughed. "Now hurry up and go. You have more vaccines in Exam Room One, and what looks like a dog that stepped on something and got his nail caught in Room Two. Easy. Chop-chop if you wanna go get the girl." Toni gave him two little claps to get him moving, and that he did.

All-business, he gave the kittens their shots and a quick check-up, then headed over to the dog. Turned out that Homer the bulldog had gotten into some firewood and got his paw cut trying to pull a log down to chew on it. Quickly cleaning and dressing the wound, Donovan got Homer all fixed up and on his way home.

As soon as the patients left, Donovan grabbed his keys. "Thank you for taking care of this," he said, gesturing at the office.

"You're welcome." She smiled at him and sat down at her desk. "Now, go. I'm sure she's pissed. Don't be above groveling. It's for the greater good."

"Got it!" he replied, jogging out the door.

Donovan raced home to let his dogs out, the only downside to being a doggie dad. When he pulled up, he saw something on his porch but couldn't quite make it out. As he got out and walked to the door, he realized it was his hoodie. The one he'd given Riley to wear. His favorite one.

Fuck.

He tucked it under his arm, then headed in the house quickly to let the dogs out and feed them. He'd tried texting and calling her already, and at the risk of making matters worse, he decided that talking to her in person was the best route to take. All he knew in that moment of pure desperation, was that he couldn't let her go without a fight.

Once his dogs and cats were taken care of, he took the hoodie with him and made the short drive to her house. On her doorstep, he knocked aggressively until Bernard opened the door.

"Dr. Hunter?" he asked.

"Where is she? I need to talk to her," he replied, almost out of breath.

"She's not here," Bernard said.

"Where did she go?" he said, despair in his voice.

"She's back in the city."

"What? Why did you let her go?" Donovan demanded.

"It's her choice, Dr. Hunter. I can't make her stay here," he replied.

"I need to get her back. Will you tell me where to find her?"

DONOVAN FOUND himself on the highway not moments later, pushing his luck for a speeding ticket. He tried calling her again, but now her phone was going straight to voicemail. Tossing his on the passenger seat, it landed on the hoodie.

What the fuck am I doing?

Two hours could be no time at all, or it could be a snail's pace when you're desperate to tell someone how you feel about them. Donovan was losing his mind driving into the city, immediately remembering why he wasn't a fan and why people didn't have cars there. The entire ride, he found himself talking out loud, trying to sort out exactly how to make her come back. How to convince her to be with him.

When he finally made it to Columbus Circle, a hotel across the street from her building allowed him to valet his car for a hefty tip so he didn't have to find parking which, at that time of day, could take an hour. Critical moments were slipping by as the pit in his stomach grew, and he went over what he wanted to say in his head.

Racing up the stairs of the walk-up, he made it to her floor like he was trying to put a fire out. Almost panting, he took a few deep breaths before aggressively knocking on her door. The loud barking would have woken the entire building if it were later. He could hear her inside, telling Scrappy to quiet down and get back, getting louder as she got closer to the door. Certain his heart would pound out of his chest, he grinned when she opened the door.

Her jaw fell open and, without a sound, she started to shut the door, when Donovan caught it. "Please don't shut me out, Riley. Let me explain," he begged.

Rolling her eyes, she opened the door for him to enter and waved him in. "What do you want, Donovan? I'm busy."

"Nothing happened with that patient... owner. Whatever. Nothing happened with Mrs. Aldridge. She's always trying to hit on me, but I swear to you, nothing happened." He spit it all out so fast he was repeating himself.

"You don't owe me an explanation, Donovan. We hardly know each other," she replied curtly.

"Don't say that, Riley. You know that isn't true. We've talked about everything. Our habits, our parents, our jobs... I do know you. I know you were happy when we were together." He stepped forward, closing the gap between them. "Why did you leave Port Henry?" he asked.

"I needed to get some stuff," she replied.

"Wait, you're going back?" he asked, stunned.

"Yeah, I was gonna wait til morning and let Scrappy stay with me, but of course I was gonna go back. Did you think I left for good?" She grinned. "Is that why you drove all the way to the city?"

"Why are you smiling?" he asked, confused.

"You drove to the city to stop me from leaving?"

"No," he said, smirking.

"Oh no? Then why?" she asked coyly.

"You forgot this," he said, handing her the hoodie.

She took the hoodie from him, lifting it to her face and inhaling with closed eyes. He might have given it a squirt of his cologne on the way up, just for good measure. Tossing it on the couch next to Scrappy, she lunged into his arms, allowing him to kiss her as passionately as he had on the beach.

Within moments, they were grabbing at each other's clothes. He pulled her shirt up over her head, revealing a white lace bra that just barely covered her tightened nipples. He slowed down for a moment, taking her in, rubbing his thumbs over them as her breath hitched at his touch. Not wanting to waste another moment, he lifted her up and, with her direction, carried her to the bedroom.

"You don't want your dog to see this," he said, chuckling.

"Oh no?" she replied, licking at his neck.

"Definitely not." He kissed her again, deeper this time, pulling her body tight to his and walking them toward the bed. Laying her down gently, he took his shirt off the rest of the way, revealing his toned chest and abs to her.

"Come here," she whispered, sprawled on the bed, still in her jeans and bra.

He kneeled next to the bed, unbuttoning her pants while

kissing at her sides, and then her hips as he slid the fabric down to her ankles before yanking them off, leaving her in a bra and panties. Before taking his pants off, he whispered, "Are you sure this is what you want?"

"I'm sure," she whispered. "Lose the pants. Now."

Not one to be told to do something important twice, he did as ordered with a smirk. Getting into the bed with her, he attempted to slow things down, wanting it to be more perfect, more romantic, for her.

"Donovan, we can do romance another time. I want you to take me right now," she demanded.

Shocked, and completely turned on, the only problem was protection. He didn't have any on him. "I don't have…"

"Top drawer," she said, pointing to her right.

He reached over and grabbed the condom from the drawer, wondering when the last time another man was in her bed. A possessive streak suddenly came out, and he wanted to claim her as his. Make her forget anyone else was ever there. He scanned over her body, lying beneath him in nothing but white lace, the rise and fall of her chest rapid with her breathing.

"Please," she urged him.

He removed his boxer briefs, slid the condom on, and hovered above her. "Tell me what you want, Riley," he demanded softly.

"I want you," she said, pulling at him.

Donovan reached down between her legs, pushing her panties to the side so he could massage her clit gently. Immediately, she arched her back and gasped as he slid one finger in, then a second, rubbing her clit with his thumb. His cock ached to be inside her, but torturing her in this way was so fucking hot.

"Tell me what you want," he demanded again, more gruffly this time.

Struggling to catch her breath, she repeated her answer. "I want you," she breathed out as she rode his fingers.

"No, tell me what you want me to do, Riley," he said, applying the slightest bit of pressure with his thumb. He wanted to taste her there, but it would have to wait. He was certain neither of them could last long enough for that.

"I want you to fuck me, Donovan!" she called out loudly, panting.

He pulled his fingers away and positioned himself over her. Lining himself up, he thrust into her wet core, groaning with pleasure. "Fuck!" he yelled out.

She wriggled her hips, and whispered, "Fuck me, Donovan Hunter. Now!"

He pulled the cups of her bra down, taking a nipple in his mouth as he thrust in and out of her, groaning in unison with her moans. As he sucked harder on one, he gently pinched the other, causing her to gasp, and he could feel her pussy tighten around his rock hard cock.

As much as he wanted to fuck her into oblivion right there, he was so close himself, and her moans were driving him wild. He could tell she had a dominant side after this moment, and rolled them over so that she was on top, riding him. She grinned, seating herself deep, and she began to lift herself up and down, sliding along his cock, her tits jiggling in rhythm. Her arms were raised above and behind her head, in the sexiest pose he'd ever seen, as if she were dancing just for him.

He reached up, taking a handful of each of her tits, rolling over her nipples with his thumbs and gently squeezing. She began to rock harder, building momentum as he continued to play with her tight little nipples. He'd found her most sensitive spot, and as he pinched them just a bit harder, she cried out, leaning forward and holding onto the headboard for leverage as she fucked him as hard as she could.

Desperate to taste her, he pulled a nipple into his mouth and sucked while she wrapped an arm around his head, balancing herself by gripping the headboard as he slammed into her, meeting her thrust for thrust. Moaning and screaming out until they both released together.

CHAPTER 24

RILEY

She knew he could be romantic. The moment they had on the beach was perfect, and driving to the city in and of itself was a grand gesture. It was obvious they were compatible. What Riley didn't need was to be pandered to, treated like she was soft and breakable. She wanted to be devoured, and that's exactly what Donovan did.

"That was incredible," he said, pulling her close.

"Mmhmm," she replied.

"Can we stay here tonight?" he asked.

"Do you want to?" she countered thoughtfully.

"I want to sleep next to you, just like this." He kissed the top of her head, which was laying on his chest.

"I'd like that," she replied. Yawning, she wrapped an arm around him and drifted off into a blissful, satiated sleep.

. . .

THE NEXT MORNING, after Scrappy was fed, they took a shower together that lasted longer than any shower normally would. Unable to keep their hands off each other, they spent the early morning getting to know every inch of each other. When they'd finally satisfied each other numerous times, slow and fast, loudly and quietly, Donovan helped her pack up the things she wanted to bring back to Port Henry.

"So, does this mean you're going to stay?" he asked hopefully.

Grinning, she asked, "Would you like me to stay?"

"Riley Maxwell, nothing would make me happier."

"I want to go back, but I don't know what's going to happen. There are some things I need to tell you."

"That sounds ominous," he replied.

"It's not about us," she said.

Donovan walked over to the couch, pulling her down on his lap. "Tell me what's going on."

Saying it out loud made it real, and she struggled to find the words. "I've been going through Jameson's things at the house."

"Of course. Did you find something?" he asked, genuine concern in his voice.

"I did," she said, taking a deep breath.

"What is it?"

"I found a picture of Jameson." She paused, preparing herself for the confession. "With my mom."

"What?"

"I found a stack of old photos in a locked drawer, and when I was going through them, I saw one that looked familiar. I took a closer look. It's definitely Jameson and my mom, at the beach, together."

"Together how?" he asked.

"Together, together. Like a couple," she said.

"Whoa," he replied.

"Yeah, but here's the thing. The first night you came over, that's the night I found it. I tucked it back in the drawer and went to hang out with you. When I went back for the picture, it was gone."

"Did you ask Bernard about it?"

"I didn't. Things have been kind of weird with him ever since he caught me snooping in Jameson's old room. Which, by the way, has been completely remodeled since he died. Which was only a week or so ago. None of his things are there, per his wishes, apparently."

"Do you think Bernard knows something?" Donovan asked.

"I do. He said that it wasn't the right time, and that he had specific instructions from Jameson on things that he'd share with me when the time *was* right."

"Well I think you need to ask him about the photo. Especially since it disappeared."

"I think you're right, but I've been too nervous about what it means."

"What do you think it means?" he asked.

"I think that Jameson had some kind of a relationship with my mom a long time ago, and for whatever reason, that's why he hired me. It wasn't because I was the best writer for his memoirs, it's because he wanted to be close to me."

"Wow," he said. "I'm fucking speechless."

"Yeah, so the other day, when I accidentally forgot to call you back, that was what happened."

Donovan squeezed her, then planted a soft kiss on her lips. "I totally understand, babe, don't worry about that. What we need to do is find out the truth though. Do you want me to go with you to ask Bernard? You know, for moral support?"

"Oh my God, would you?" she asked.

"Of course." He grinned and took her hand in his. "Riley, I want to be with you. That means here, there, wherever. You were literally sent to me from the heavens or something. I had no idea what I was missing until you came into the Rusty Scupper like a goddamn tornado, and I wanna get caught up in your storm, wherever it leads."

Riley blushed, not knowing what to say. It was the kindest, most romantic thing anyone had ever said to her. "Thank you," she replied softly, leaning into him for a kiss. Not a sexy, passionate kiss, but a loving, tender kiss, full of promise and new beginnings.

"What do you say you and me and Scrappy head back, and we'll go talk to Bernard. Together."

"I'd like that very much." Riley then remembered that she and Scrappy had driven there themselves. "Ugh. I drove here. So what am I gonna do with my other car?"

Donovan laughed. "Well, you *are* rich. Just have someone deliver it back to you at the Port."

"I am pretty rich." She laughed. "You have a rich girlfriend. I guess that means I'm your sugar mama." She started laughing even harder, a fit of giggles taking over.

"So, you're my girlfriend?" he asked, raising an eyebrow at her.

Riley stopped giggling, worried she'd jumped the gun and presumed too much. "Uh—" She hesitated, and Donovan started laughing.

"Of course you are," he teased her. "Know what that means?"

Confused, she replied, "All the hoodies that smell like you are mine now?"

"Haha! Close. It means I'm your boyfriend." He pulled her in for one more kiss before lifting them both up to go.

I have a boyfriend. A hot boyfriend. A hot, animal doctor boyfriend. What is this life?

CHAPTER 25

DONOVAN

Donovan and his *girlfriend* drove back to Port Henry in his Escalade, discussing what Jameson's connection to her might be. They ran into quite a bit of traffic, both in the city and along the highway to the beach. Summer season was starting. Grateful she wouldn't be taking up commuting back and forth like many New Yorkers did, he reached over the console and took her hand in his, gently rubbing his thumb across her hand.

"Do you think you're related somehow?" he asked.

"I have no idea, I guess that's possible?" she replied questioningly.

"Maybe he and your mom were old college friends, and since he didn't have any kids and knew that your mom passed away, he wanted you to be his benefactor?"

"Hmm, that could be," she said thoughtfully, staring out

the window as they crawled in traffic. "Is traffic always this bad?"

"Yes, it is. That's why I hate coming into the city, except at Christmastime," he replied.

"Is there less traffic then?" she asked, sounding confused.

"No, not at all, but Christmas in the city is beautiful. I love how the whole town is decorated, and it's got a much softer glow than the usual harshness I get from it." Donovan reminisced about the season; both he and his mother were Christmas junkies. They loved everything about it, and Christmas at the Port was fun too. But over the years, Donovan and his mom would go see *The Nutcracker* or Radio City Music Hall's *Christmas Spectacular* show as it got closer to the actual holiday.

"You're right, it is beautiful in the winter. Right now though, it's getting hot and dirty," she said with a small chuckle.

"Just one more reason it's a good thing you're staying in the Port." He brought her hand to his lips, placing a gentle kiss there. "What made you decide you were going to stay, really?" he asked, curious what the deciding factor was.

"Even though I found myself here on sad pretenses, I've been happy there. Relaxed. My best friend came down from Boston the other day and reminded me that I don't have to make any decisions now, and I also don't have to get back to work. Jameson was my only client. I have all the time in the world now, to figure out where I want to be and what I want to do next."

Fishing, he asked her, "I mean, you have a boyfriend here now, so you should probably stay for him too, because he'd be devastated if you left."

She glanced over at him as he smirked, an affectionate

grin on her face. "I do have a boyfriend now. Free hoodies foreverrr..." She dragged the word out, laughing.

"Babe, you can take anything you want as long as you promise to keep laughing like that." The sound of her laugh was like music and it lifted him in a way he couldn't quite describe. But with her, he felt lighter. "I mean I'd also take some more of last night. And this morning," he added, squeezing her hand.

"That was a delicious shower, wasn't it," she replied wistfully.

"Mmhmm," he replied. Donovan had never experienced shower sex, and realized in an instant, with Riley bent over in front of him and the water raining around them, that he had been missing out. They had gone from passionate and desperate for each other, to loving, demanding every inch to be kissed or touched, to downright hot and almost filthy. His cock started to twitch thinking about how beautiful and smart she was coupled with her voracious appetite for sex with him. *If this is what a relationship is all about, I've been missing out. Maybe your subconscious was just waiting on her to show up.*

They finally arrived in front of her house, and not a moment too soon. After they let Scrappy out of the vehicle, he immediately ran to water the plants and then ran around the front yard like a maniac, stretching his long legs. It was a long car ride, but with the traffic, it could be brutal.

They stood in the yard, watching Scrappy for a few minutes, before Donovan grabbed her hand. "You ready?"

"I think so? I'm just gonna tell him that I'm not leaving until he tells me what is going on," she replied. "He needs to tell me why Jameson wanted me here and what the picture of my mom is all about."

"Okay, good. Go team," he said. "I'll be here the whole

time. Be brave." He pulled her in for a quick embrace, kissing the top of her head before they went inside. "When we're done and you have some answers, we can take a nap together. I'm still exhausted, how about you?"

"That sounds perfect. And maybe a little more... you know?" She grinned.

"I do know. And making love to my girlfriend on my day off all day sounds fucking perfect." He loved saying it. In fact, he loved it so much, he wanted to drag her all over town introducing her as such. *His girlfriend.*

Riley flashed him a huge smile.

Holding on to Riley's hand, he could sense how nervous she was. Her palm was slightly sweaty, and he could feel her pulse quickening just slightly.

They made it inside, Scrappy running along too, probably thinking he'd get a second breakfast. Bernard was sitting in his usual spot, sipping a cup of coffee and reading the *Sunday Times*.

"Bernard?" Riley said.

Grinning, he glanced between the two, landing on their clasped hands. "Good morning, Riley, Dr. Hunter. What can I do for you two? Would you like breakfast?"

Donovan almost said yes, he'd had Bernard's cooking before, but he had to stay on task. Be a supportive boyfriend. He grinned at himself.

"Everything okay, Dr. Hunter?" Bernard asked.

"Oh, uh yes. Sorry. No, we don't need breakfast, but thank you very much for offering." Donovan squeezed Riley's hand so she would say something; he was getting nervous himself.

Finally, Riley jumped in. "Bernard, I'd like to speak with you about the photograph I found of my mother in Jameson's desk. I think you know the one."

Giving his full attention to the beautiful woman, he nodded. "I am familiar with at least one such picture." He smiled.

"Why did Jameson Prescott have a photograph of my mother from what looked like thirty years ago? Why did it disappear? Were they friends and that's why he left me everything, because he didn't have any kids of his own?"

Riley began rapid-firing questions at Bernard, not letting him answer one before she had asked another. Donovan leaned in and whispered, "Baby, give him a chance to answer."

"Oh, yeah. You're right," she muttered. Turning back to Bernard, she apologized, "I'm sorry, Bernard, I haven't given you a chance to speak."

"It's fine, Riley, I know that you have a lot of questions. And, I told you when the time was right, you'd get some answers." He placed his hands one on top of the other. "Let me ask you something, Riley?"

Confused, she replied, "Of course, what is it?"

"Do you intend to stay here, in Port Henry? Maybe not forever, but for the foreseeable future? Are you now planning to make this your home?" he asked.

Donovan waited with bated breath to hear her answer. They had talked about it, but that was just between them. Admitting it to the world was big, and he couldn't wait.

She grinned, glancing over at Donovan before answering. "I am. As you can see, Dr. Hunter and I are seeing each other. He is my boy– He's my boyfriend, and I'm staying here. And yes, I'm keeping Scrappy, before you even ask. That dumb dog is my other best friend. Why are you asking?"

Bernard got up from his seat and walked across the kitchen, opening a drawer near the edge of the counter. He pulled a small stack of photos out, and an envelope with her name on it. "One of the stipulations for revealing what I'm about to tell you was that you had to be committed to staying in Port Henry for an extended period of time, making it your full-time home."

"Stipulations?" she asked.

"You knew Jameson. He liked things done his way. But, you have fulfilled your end of the deal even though you didn't know about it. So, I do have some answers for you." He handed her the pictures, causing her to gasp. Over and over.

"What is it?" Donovan asked frantically.

"Bernard, what is going on here. Why do you have all these pictures of my mom?" she asked, gently waving them in front of her.

"Those pictures belonged to your father," he replied softly.

"My father? But how do you know my father?"

Donovan watched as it hit her like a ton of bricks. His own jaw dropping as he made the connection, he waited for her reaction.

"Jameson Prescott *was* your father."

THE END... FOR NOW.

Stay tuned for the continuing story of Riley, Donovan, and their friends in Port Henry, coming soon.

Love in the Midwest (Novella Duet)

Christmas With You (a Holiday Anthology)

Jordyn's Army (an Anthology)

One Hot Summer (an Anthology)

ABOUT THE AUTHOR

Formerly a firefighter and EMT in New Jersey, Amy Briggs grew up next to a military base, which inspires many of her stories. Amy draws on her experiences in emergency services to show the depth and emotional side of the lifestyle. Her love of fairy tales carries through each of her novels and she hopes to inspire readers to fall in love with love. Amy lives in Texas with her family and more cats than she can handle.

Amy loves to hear from readers and can be found on all the social media here: www.facebook.com/amybriggsauthor, Instagram @amybriggs23 & on Twitter at @amybriggs23. You can also email her at amy@amybriggsauthor.com

Find a full list of all of Amy Briggs books at: www.amybriggsauthor.com

Made in the USA
Las Vegas, NV
28 August 2024